Masked Love

RON FEATHERINGILL
DAVID HALDANE

Copyright © 2024 by Ron Featheringill and David Haldane

All rights reserved.

No part of this book may be reproduced in any form or by any electronic or mechanical means, including information storage and retrieval systems, without written permission from the author, except for the use of brief quotations in a book review.

Dedication

To the authors' long-suffering wives, Bonnie Slavik and Ivy Haldane, and Ron's two grown children, Scott Featheringill and Lynette Jones.

"An author ought to write for the youth of his own generation, the critics of the next, and the schoolmaster ever afterward."
    F. Scott Fitzgerald

Chapter One

Sometimes I hate my brother. If I'm honest, the feeling is probably not hatred but jealousy. The thing I really resent is his being so "perfect." It's not that he does nothing wrong, because he does. It's just that he can get himself into almost any scrape and come out smelling like a rose. When I try doing that, I get caught and into serious trouble. Like the trouble I'm in now. My brother, on the other hand, could probably do the exact same thing and convince everyone that it's perfectly all right.

There was one thing I had over him. He's a year younger than me, and I was going to graduate first and find my way in the "real world," so to speak. Now all that has changed. If I can get my life back together, it will take me at least another year to graduate. My brother, on the other hand, has gained early admission to Stanford with a full scholarship based on academic *and* athletic ability. He and Dad won't have to pay a penny for his education because Stanford expects him to suit up for Frosh football. They also expect him to get good grades, and he probably will. Even if I wanted to go to college—which I'm not sure I do anymore—I probably wouldn't get in because my grades are so bad. I thought about going to a junior college, but now that I have to repeat my senior year and follow in my little brother's footsteps, I probably will look for a job after graduation. If I ever graduate, that is. It doesn't really matter because, to tell the truth, I've had enough school. It is *so* boring. And my brother's act is hard to follow.

Another thing that bugs me about him is that he's almost too good-looking. I don't know where he got his good looks because Dad and I certainly don't have them. My brother is movie-star good-looking, if you know what I mean. My mother died when I was five, and I've seen pictures of her. I suppose she was a pretty woman, but it's sure hard to judge your own mother's beauty. My brother might have gotten his looks from her. I know my brother is attractive because of the way girls act around him. They always act gushy, and tell me, "Gee, your brother looks *so* good!" Whenever we're together, the girls see only him, never me. I really hate that. It's always the same whenever he and I go to a store or the movies. The girls turn their heads to look at him. He's so handsome, he's almost pretty. Even middle-aged women and old ladies look at him, yet he never seems to notice. I always feel like a nonentity around him. Since I changed the way I look and dress, people look at me too now. But most of them do it only because they think I'm weird. Some girls find me attractive, I guess, but they're usually screwed up with lots of problems and I'm not too crazy about them. I'll tell you more about that later.

The thing I really don't understand about my brother is his attitude towards women. I mean, if I had all the opportunities he does, I'd be dangerous and probably in a lot more trouble than I am right now, though that's hard to imagine. Regarding sex, my brother is really a prude. He once told me that even if a really beautiful girl begged him to go to bed with her, he'd say no. He says he likes to kiss girls and hold them tight and dance with them and all, but he won't even try to feel them up because it might lead to making love. He's afraid that once he gets started, he won't be able to stop. Getting a girl pregnant, he says, would ruin him. He'd have to drop out of school. And besides, he tells me, there are all kinds of bad venereal diseases out there and more teenagers have them than anyone can imagine, because some of the diseases take so long to show up. He is determined not to let disease or pregnancy ruin his life. And the way he can be sure of that is by not going too far with a girl.

I don't know where he gets ideas like this. Neither me nor my dad is stuck in all this puritan crap. Our family has never hung out at church. Since my mother died, my father has gone with some "girls" as he calls them. He doesn't tell us about all the dirty things he does with them. But he doesn't deny doing way more than holding hands, either. He never preaches at me or my brother. In fact, he tells us that sex and God are two of the greatest mysteries the world will ever know and that each man must come to terms with them as best he can. I guess my brother sucked his attitudes out of his own thumb, because he was only four when Mom died. Maybe my brother's ideas have something to do with his being so extraordinarily good-looking. They say that men who are too good-looking are kind of funny, if you know what I mean. Like Brad Pitt and Leonardo DiCaprio. My dad used to like a guy named Rock Hudson, who was very handsome and very gay. He even died of AIDS, poor guy. I've seen none of his movies, though the name "Hudson" sends shivers up my spine, and you will soon find out why. I really wonder about my brother, and that's why I'm telling you this story. You'll have to decide for yourself.

There is one field where my brother has nothing over me, and that's in athletic ability. I seem to have an unusual knack for catching a football, and I just finished a rather brilliant season (if I may say so myself) as the starting left end on our high school football team. They even awarded me first-team all-league honors for breaking the school record in touchdowns and total yards gained for a receiving end. My brother is not a shabby player either and made first-team all-league as a running back. He also has a full athletic scholarship to Stanford, as I said earlier, even though he will only be a senior in high school next year. However, because of my poor grades, I will probably never put my athletic ability to use unless something good happens to me. Right now, I can't imagine what that would be.

In fact, right now, I'm not really doing anything. I have a job at a gas station, and for the past couple of weeks I've been driving up here to visit an old buddy in his apartment near the University of California. He used to go to my old high school, and now he goes to U.C. Santa Barbara. He's nice enough to let me stay with him, but thinks I have a negative attitude and am not using my talents, whatever they are. People like him drive me up a wall because they think if you don't go to college, you're wasting your life. I like this guy just fine, although he bugs me.

And I can't deny that he's nice not to charge me any rent when my finances aren't too great.

You might wonder why I'm up here and just what I'm doing. The answer is simple, although nobody believes me. I'm in love. I love a girl named Lisa and have loved her for an entire year. In fact, I fell in love with her the minute I saw her picture. Like you see in the movies or read about in the old romance novels. My brother, the S.O.B., tells me I don't have the "capacity" to love anyone sincerely and that, knowing me as he does, I am "in lust" not in love. He says I'm such an animal that I don't know the difference between those two things. He may be right because I actually see little difference between love and sex, and he says that's what makes me an animal. I have asked him to explain the difference because he says he knows what it is. He has many neat little expressions like, "A woman gives sex to get love, and a man gives love to get sex," which I don't find convincing at all. And I tell him it's his problem that he looks at things like a woman would because maybe he's trans or queer or bisexual or something. But he doesn't get mad. He just tells me he isn't gay or anything and that a real man doesn't have to prove he's a stud all the time. In fact, in order to irritate me, he says he's worried about me because of the way I go for blood if someone, even indirectly, questions my sexuality. If I were more secure in my masculinity and didn't doubt it myself, he says, I wouldn't have beaten up that kid last year who called me a fag because I had a pierced ear. My brother's logical way of arguing and the way he twists everything around really pisses me off. Sometimes I'd like to beat him within an inch of his life, and I would try it if I was sure I could walk away with no bruises myself. Besides, my father would kill me. He tells me over and over that Paul (that's my brother's name) has most of the brains in the family and that we should all be proud of him. It's not that my father is partial to Paul, it's just that Paul seems to be moving in a positive direction that none of us should interfere with. This doesn't mean I don't have any brains or a chance for a wonderful future, my father tells me, just that my talents (expect my sports ability) lie in another area, and my course in life seems different. I can't get mad at my father for telling me these things, because he's right. I really love my father (I wonder what Paul would say about my love for Dad), and really don't think he loves Paul more than he does me. He just appreciates our differences and doesn't condemn me because I always get in trouble.

The word "trouble" makes me remember what I was telling you; that I love Lisa, but no one believes me. Wait, that isn't quite right because I think Lisa believes me, or at least she used to. And, really, that's all that matters, isn't it? The word "trouble" also jars my memory because that's what I got Lisa into. I'm sorry, but that's the truth, and I'm not trying to hide anything now. If I were fruity like my brother, probably Lisa and I would be better off. I will never admit that to him, of course. Right now, Lisa is in a home for "unwed" mothers in a rather impressive-looking area just south of Santa Barbara. I forget the name of the place, but the area is green even though it doesn't get much rain. The houses around there take your breath away. You can't help but wonder what people do to live in houses like those. There are expensive cars everywhere, and gardeners. A thick hedge surrounds the place where Lisa stays. There is really no way through it unless you have a pair of heavy-duty wire cutters. I guess you can tell that I've tried crawling through the hedge by what I'm telling you now. An almost invisible chain-link fence stopped me. Not to mention the devilish barbed wire woven through the fence and crowning it on top. Besides, the place is crawling with guards and dogs. I guess all those precautions keep guys like me away. When I go up to a better vantage point atop the hill, I can see that the white building looks like some attractive estate house and the grounds have well-kept green lawns and lovely gardens and walkways. So far, I've seen nothing of Lisa, even though I've roamed the area several hours every weekend for over three months now. This place must cost Lisa's dad a bundle. But the guy's made of money, and the expense probably doesn't hurt him a bit. I know he's pissed about Lisa, and I guess I can't really blame him. This story's so long and complicated, I may as well start from the beginning.

Chapter Two

I can't believe all this started less than a year ago because it seems like ages have passed, especially during the last couple of months. My brother and I used to go to a high school on the west side of town, but my father heard of all the problems caused by drugs and gangs at the school and insisted that we move to a nicer section of the city to attend a better school. Paul and I really had very little trouble because we were outstanding athletes and started on the football and baseball teams. Paul started as a running back in varsity football, even though he was just a sophomore. This is a distinction I can't claim because I played JV football as a sophomore. Anyway, because Paul and I were athletes, the gangs didn't bother us much. Not that we were in a wonderful neighborhood—there were lots of gangsters around committing lots of crimes—but somehow, they seemed to respect our playing ability and left us alone. Some of them were even sort of our friends. Until I made the mistake of messing with one of them, as I will tell you later.

Drugs were a real problem at the high school. You could get just about any kind of drug you wanted. Even though many students I knew were pushers, I tried nothing more serious than a little pot and didn't even like it. I'm sure Paul never touched the stuff. But then the cops pulled off a major drug bust on campus and several of our friends (some of them football players) got hauled in. When Dad saw the story all over the local paper, he said enough was enough and moved us again, this time to a sleepy little community down by the beach. We've never owned a place of our own because my father doesn't make enough money. Because we've always rented, though, it wasn't hard to pack up everything and move to another apartment..

What my dad still doesn't know, though, is that things are the same at this new high school. Paul and I have no major problem making friends because we do pretty well on the football team here, too, and Paul is an outstanding baseball player as well. In fact, they elected Paul junior class president this year. But drugs are everywhere, just like at our old high school. The gangsters at the new place are not as hard-core, and most are "wannabes." The real gangs are definitely moving in, though, because there are so many clean-cut middle-class kids who have nothing better to do with all their dough than buy drugs. One teacher told us last year that drugs are so prevalent in the so-called "bad section" of town that the price has gone down. So, the dealers are extending their territory into more affluent areas where they can make better money. In fact, what they're really doing is "establishing franchises." At least that's what it's called when MacDonald's does the same thing.

Another reason my brother and I have no trouble at the new high school is because people think of us as "nice" Mexicans. Paul doesn't even really look Hispanic. He's so clean-cut and nice-looking that most people think he's Italian. They don't know what to think of me, though, because I like the punk style and punk music too. You've probably heard of it; maybe your dad and mom were into it back in their day. Anyway, even though it's a throwback, I wear black leather, chains, and earrings. I listen to the music and would go miles to hear a concert, though there aren't too many of them around anymore. But anyone who knows me knows I don't like to fight (although I won't run away from one) and am not mean or violent. I suppose I draw their attention because I'm Hispanic and most punks aren't. People stop to take a second look and discover that I'm not vicious. I look like a punk, true, but don't hang out with other punks, probably because there aren't too many of them around anymore. My friends come in all races, colors and creeds and most of them have been pretty good about not stereotyping me. I can't help but hear what some of them say, though. I've heard people say I'm a punk, *but* very nice and friendly. Or that I'm a Mexican, but a *nice* one. I don't enjoy hearing comments like that, but I know these people mean well and wish me no harm. Everyone seems so sensitive these days that it's hard to say anything without offending someone. I don't feel like I'm discriminated against racially because I really look like a punker more than a Mexican. I'm not saying other people don't get hassled because of their race, though. It just doesn't happen much to me, and I'm sure Paul would say the same thing.

Anyway, we'd just finished a hard day during "Hell Week." Hell Week isn't exactly an accurate expression because football try-outs before school opens last way longer than a week. They feel like pure hell, though, especially now that they make us wear masks because of this stupid COVID thing that's going around. When we were done with practice, I'd always rip the mask off as fast as I could, then remove my shoulder pads and ring the sweat out from the tee shirt under my pads. I'll never forget that drinking fountain near the tennis courts because the water was so cool and pleasant, and it seemed like you could just stand there drinking that cool water for half an hour. It sure was great getting the dirt and sweat off in the showers. I remember standing at the shower head drinking the cool water for what seemed like forever. I remember doing that on the day the gym opened for the first time. Until then, the entire school was off limits to us, except for the locker room and the football field. I'm a pretty cocky guy, and when I discovered the gym was open, I wanted to see the trophy case because most high schools post their school records there. I wanted to see if there were any records in football, track or baseball that I might have a shot at in the coming year.

But while I was looking at the trophy case, I saw a picture of the pep squad for the year. This was also one of things I wanted to see because I always like to check out the finer chicks so maybe I can score in that area too. Well, thank God, the girls had posed for this year's picture without their masks and, as I looked, a particular girl grabbed my attention. She seemed to have a radiance that the others lacked. I couldn't take my eyes off her! It was like the other members of the pep squad didn't even exist.

Just then I felt someone's presence coming towards me, but pretended not to notice and kept gazing at the picture that had grabbed my attention.

"I knew you were a lecher, Santos," a voice behind me said. It was Coach Miller, who was a new student teacher helping with the varsity football team. He was a pretty good line coach who had a respectable record of his own playing football at the local State University.

"Hi Coach," I said, still looking at the photograph. "Do you know who the girl is here on the lower left-hand side of this picture?"

"Which one?" he asked, bending closer to look.

"This one right here." I pointed again so there would be no mistake.

"That's Lisa Hudson," Miller said. "I can see you have good taste, Santos, but I think you're a bit too old for Lisa here. She's just a sophomore. And besides, you might as well kiss her off. Her father has her watched night and day and won't let her out of his sight when she's not at school. It's obviously *verboten* for her to date until she graduates in about three years. By then, you'll probably have found somebody else to stare at."

It surprised me that she was a sophomore. Let me try to put it nicely. She was radiant and beautiful, and her face reflected the intelligent maturity that you rarely see in high school sophomores. So many of those girls are just frizzy-haired airheads. And I surely haven't seen too many sophomores with well-developed bodies like this girl had. Even now, as I stand on this hill, just thinking of Lisa's lovely breasts makes me want to cry. I guess that's why my brother insists I'm an animal.

"But Coach, how can a father prevent his daughter from going out until she graduates from high school?" I wanted to know. "Don't you think that's unreasonable? It's not the Dark Ages but the 21st century in the land of the free and home of the brave and all that."

I paused before continuing.

"And besides," I said, "how do you know so much about this Lisa girl, anyway? I saw you at the movies last week with a woman that looked like your girlfriend, remember? Don't you realize you're not supposed to know things about other girls, especially when they're minors?"

"Listen, Santos," the coach said. "I've always believed that just because you're on a diet doesn't mean you can't look at the menu. And not only that, but I'm just 21 and the girls down here don't look too bad to me. They're not much younger than me."

Now it was his tun to pause.

"You won't tell anyone I said that, will you, Santos?" the coach finally continued. "There's got to be some added benefits to this job

9

because there's sure no money in it. But if you give me any lip, I won't tell you what I know about Lisa."

He turned to leave the foyer.

"Come on, Coach!" I begged, seriously now. "If you know more about this girl, please tell me. I really have to know."

"Well, what do you want to know, Santos?" Miller asked, seeming serious himself now.

"Here I've met the woman of my dreams, and you tell me she's off limits. How do you know that?"

"Let's just say I take an interest in Lisa and her sister, the girl over there on the other side of the picture," Miller responded.

I didn't look at the picture because, if Lisa had a sister, I already knew I wasn't interested. I'm not even sure I heard the coach. "Please cut out this guessing game and tell me what you know?" I pleaded.

"OK Santos, but let's make it quick. The lady you saw me with is waiting for me right now because, frankly, I enjoy playing cards. It's my one vice. You won't tell anyone, will you, Santos?"

When I assured him I wouldn't, he confessed that once a week he played cards with Alihandro, who worked as a gardener for Lisa's dad, as well as a few other friends. Though none of them were serious gamblers, Miller said they enjoyed the game. And while he usually beat Alihandro, he always returned the money by buying toys for the gardener's kids or helping other Nicaraguans serving as domestics in the Hudson household. Rich people often hire Nicaraguans to help with household chores, Miller said. The only problem was that Alihandro's wife had arrived in the US with the children earlier through an amnesty program, while her husband had just walked across the border illegally. And just recently US Immigration and Customs Enforcement had gotten wind of Alihandro's presence and was hot on his trail. So it was probably just a matter of days, Miller said, until he got deported.

"You won't tell anyone about this, will you, Santos?" Miller asked again before continuing.

Then he told me that Alihandro has two favorite topics he enjoys discussing at the weekly card parties: ragging on the US Government for its inconsistent and unfair immigration policies, and telling stories about Mr. Hudson's foolishness.

According to Coach Miller, Lisa's father had many problems, the root of which was his marriage to a younger woman. Lisa's mother died when she was four, and old man Hudson busied himself right away looking for a younger replacement. It didn't take him long to find one, either, because he's filthy rich. So it isn't surprising that the lady he found turned out to be a gold digger, in it mainly for the money. Mr. Hudson's a big executive for IBM or something. I guess after a brief honeymoon period, the new Mrs. Hudson set herself up in her own bedroom and the old man has been hurting ever since, if you know what I mean. I guess Mrs. Hudson is a big hit at the country club and spends most of her time there playing tennis and golf. There are rumors she goes out with other men, but so far they're just rumors. Miller says she doesn't seem to care much about her two stepdaughters. After all, she's only a few years older than they are, probably not a day over 30. Anyway, Miller thinks that's why there's so much weirdness going on in the Hudson household. He must have majored in English because he summed it all up by quoting some old dead English poet whose name I never heard and can't remember:

"A man should pick an equal for his mate.
Youth and old age are often in debate.
However, he had fallen in the snare,
And had to bear his cross as others bear."

I DON'T KNOW IF I HAVE THAT QUITE RIGHT. I'M ALWAYS amazed at how Miller seems able to quote so much from memory. He even does it on the football field. He loves to moralize and thinks football is a metaphor for life or something like that. For such a young guy, he sure is boring. He teaches English, and everybody complains about him. Most of the guys think his habit of quoting poetry means that he's gay or something.

I'm not so sure where I stand on the matter. He was putting his hands all over that girl at the movies, kissing her on the neck and all. He doesn't seem to realize that he's supposed to act like a teacher and not some horny teenager. I don't see how he could be gay, being a football star and all, but you never know. At least that's what grownups keep telling me. I guess what people do in their own bedrooms is their own business.

Let me say this about Miller, though. I can't stand how some people look at a problem and reduce it down to one thing. Like all Hudson's troubles are about his being married to a younger woman. I'm not defending the old man. I didn't really know Mr. Hudson when Miller talked to me, and I still don't know him very well. But life is complex, if you know what I mean. You can't just sum it up in a sentence or two. People who went to college seem to get off on putting everything into one statement. Like teachers, preachers, and even some cops. Maybe that's why I'm afraid of going to college. I might end up being even more pinheaded than I am already.

Miller told me Hudson does everything he can to please his wife and get into her good graces. He buys things and sends her on expensive vacations. She keeps telling him she feels uncomfortable with his daughters in the house, girls who are close to her own age. They seem to be critical of her, always spying on her and talking behind her back and such.

The crap really hit the fan, apparently, when they had a party at the Hudson house and lots of people from the country club showed up. The tennis pro, rumored to be getting it on with Mrs. Hudson, brought an old Bill Cosby tape to see if he could piss off Mr. Hudson. And the plan worked even better than he'd hoped.

The tape is about a guy who's looking forward to seeing his daughter move out and find a place of her own so he can retire and spread his wings or do whatever retired people do. But the daughter gets pregnant and then straightens out and ends up going to college to become a lawyer or doctor or something. Because she's a student, of course, she leaves the baby with Mom and Dad. And because they're excellent parents glad that their daughter straightened out, they agree to mind the baby while she's in college. When the daughter finally graduates, though, she gives up law or medicine and becomes an anthropologist or something and goes to Africa to study her roots. So while the daughter's away for years and years with Mom and Pop receiving only occasional postcards, the granddaughter is growing up and gets pregnant in junior high school. The poor old man who was just looking to retire in life ends up running this endless babysitting agency in his own home. I'm not really sure how well I'm telling you about the Cosby tape because I've never actually heard it, and Miller heard the story from Alihandro.

As if Cosby's an authority on anything anymore now that he's in jail. All of which probably even added to old Mr. Hudson's irritation.

Anyway, what started out as a joke to get Hudson riled up ended up being a really serious problem for the whole Hudson family. Because he didn't see the humor in it and started making plans not to end up like the guy on the tape. He started keeping his daughters away from boys come hell or high water. He tore up a lot of his backyard to build a gigantic wall around the entire property. The family already lived on one of those concrete islands off the coast of Southern California that you can get to only by driving across a bridge. Alihandro started driving the girls to school in the limousine and picking them up right after afternoon cheer practice. They could be on the pep squad, but they'd better not fraternize with any of the football players! Neither one of them could date or go anywhere without Alihandro or his wife, Maria, along for the ride. I felt really sorry for Lisa. She must lead a miserable life. But I also started feeling sorry for myself, because I sort of understood Miller's point that this girl was off limits. I wondered how I was ever going to contact her.

There was only one glimmer of hope. Hudson was more worried about Lora than about her twin sister, Lisa. You would never know they were twins. They are both attractive, I can see that now. Even while Miller was talking to me, in fact, I'd looked at her picture and noticed that she wasn't bad looking at all. But they are as different as night and day. Lisa, as I told you before, is radiant, always standing out and attracting lots of attention. Lora is dark and blends into a crowd. But, as I was saying, Hudson is more worried about Lora because she's not a good student in school, getting mostly C's and Ds. I guess she's not too interested in school, sort of like me. Lisa gets nothing but A's and B's and doesn't seem interested in guys at all. Lora strikes that old man as being boy-crazy, and Hudson is afraid she'll end up pregnant with no husband or future. But Miller thinks Hudson doesn't know his own daughters. While it's true that Lisa does well in school, he says, there's a mischievous spark in her eye; a plain sign she might play if the right guy comes along. And though Lora gets poor grades and talks a lot about boys, there's a hardheaded reasonableness about her suggesting that she may save herself for when she gets married.

I am doing my best to paraphrase Miller here. This isn't normally the way I think, pigeonholing people the way he does. People can really act any way they want, given the right situation or stimulant. At least that's what I believe.

Anyway, about then, Miller broke off his story and started looking at his watch.

"God dammit, Santos, it's five o'clock, and here I am shooting the shit with you when I've got a date. I'd better split or I'm in deep trouble with my lady. You won't repeat what I've told you, right, Santos? If I hear you've blabbed, I'll punch your lights out. I don't give a damn if you *are* just some little high school student."

He gave me a playful punch on the shoulder, which made me glad he was kidding.

"Hey, Coach, don't you have any confidence in me?" I reassured him with a wink in my voice. "I don't talk to people about things like this. You know I'm a good end too. I'll make you look great by breaking a few records this season. I'll tell everybody you taught me how to do it."

"Yes, Michael," he said, "I know you have talent and potential, and maybe you'll really help the team this year. But seriously, keep what I've told you under your hat, will you? Hudson is a fool, but he's rich and nobody can cause you as much trouble as a rich fool. Lisa's a terrific looker, but I still think you'd be wasting your time on her. There are plenty of other girls around here. Do what you want, but if I see the girls are on your mind so much that they're affecting you're playing, you're going to hear about it. And remember, I didn't tell you anything about the Hudsons."

"You've got my word Coach," I said, "mum's the word. I really appreciate what you've told me."

"All right, Mike, I've got to go now. See ya tomorrow." And, with no further ado, he left the building.

When I was alone, I looked at Lisa's picture again. Something was happening to me that had never happened before. I was feeling this pleasant pain in my diaphragm, all excited and happy. Even though I was dead tired after my workout, I felt full of energy. I really felt that I'd fallen in love with Lisa just by looking at her picture.

That feeling hasn't changed, it's just gotten more intense over the past few months. I know you're going to think I'm just another slobbering adolescent with raging hormones, but you're wrong. There is something different about what I feel for Lisa, although I'm not very good at describing it. It's sort of like I can only think of *her.* Other girls, including her twin sister, seem dull now.

I remember that day in the foyer thinking about what Coach Miller had told me. One of the funny feelings I had was fear. It scared me that I could never meet or talk to Lisa. She might even think I was a lecher because I was two years older than her. I might not be good-looking enough for her. What if my brother saw her and got interested? He's surely hot enough for her.

The thing that bothered me most was that she was an excellent student. I had nothing in common with her there, and, here again, Paul *did*. How would I talk to her? She would probably think me a stupid fool. I know Miller said she might play if she met the right guy, but I wasn't sure I was the right guy. And besides, there seemed to be so many road blocks between me and her that it was probably unlikely I'd ever get close to her in a sexual sense.

But I was in love, and love is a challenge. I decided to think positively about all this and tell my brother what was happening. When Coach Miller opened the door to the gym foyer, I noticed Paul was still out on the street, talking to some friends.

I went over to where he was and the guys with him said hello, but I felt all excited and didn't want to add anything to their conversation. I wished these guys would bug out and leave me with Paul so that we could talk alone. Finally, after about 15 minutes, I couldn't contain myself any longer and said, "Hey, Paul, you know that we have to be home by a quarter to six, and the gym closes up at 5:30. There's something in there I want to show you."

The other guys took the hint and left, saying they'd see us later. Then Paul turned to me and said, "Hey, what's up, Mike? You know the gym closes at six, and there's nobody telling us to get home this minute."

"I know, Paul, but I've just seen the picture of the love of my life. I want you to come in to see what she looks like."

But Paul frowned and started lecturing me again. I had heard the sermon before.

"Come off it, Mike! Why are we at this new high school, anyway? It's you and girls. Always you and girls! Remember, you and I talked about this before?"

And off we went, delivering the usual lecture with new enthusiasm. Reminding me of how good we'd had it at our old school until I took up with Sandy, a girl whose pants he knew I'd get into in no time at all. And how, sure enough, I'd gotten her pregnant and taken her to LA for an abortion. And how, her being a 'home girl' and all, she had lots of brothers and 'friends' who'd decided "settle up" with me.

"Poor Dad," Paul said. "He still doesn't know the half of it. He thinks the gangsters were just picking on you for no reason when, actually, they were doing a pretty good job of leaving you alone until you started messing with them. For Crissakes, Mike, why can't you just leave the girls alone until after graduation?"

Then he reminded me that I was a high school senior just scraping by and screwing up would undoubtedly delay my graduation.

"You'll be in summer school," Paul said, "and, if you don't drop out, you'll get your diploma by mail. I wouldn't be talking to like this if you had some self-control. If you could just keep your thing to yourself, you could go out with whoever you wanted and have a good time."

Instead, he reminded me, "All you think about is sex. You're not happy unless you're having an adult relationship with a girl, even though you're only a half-witted kid. You like having fun but lack any sense of responsibility. We've talked about all this before; you promised you'd go straight at this new high school. You'd keep your mind on football and baseball and try to pull up your grades. That was our agreement, don't you remember?"

But I was way too excited to be mad at Paul. He was such a jerk; I knew he couldn't feel what I was feeling. He didn't know how to have a good time and probably never would. I even pitied him, although, as usual, he was right about a lot of things. Our old high school *had* been a pretty good setup, especially for Paul. He was really popular with everyone, including the teachers. Even as a sophomore, he had scouts coming to watch him at games. It's hard to pull up stakes and start all over again at a new place. He did that for me. It wasn't his fault. But after the thing with Sandy, the situation got pretty hairy in our neighborhood. There were only a few fights, and I didn't come out too bad because Paul was usually around to help. But tensions were building up. I had a bad feeling that something was about to happen, something I couldn't stop with my fists. I talked to Paul about it, and he agreed because he felt it too. Then my father started noticing things. He noticed that Paul and I came home pretty scraped up a couple of times and asked us why the gangsters seemed to congregate along our street when they'd never done that before. We didn't really tell him anything except that the gangs were getting stronger in our neighborhood, and the gangsters were becoming more visible. My father isn't one to interrogate you, but this was all he needed to know. About a week later, he announced we were moving, as I told you before.

Paul and I have had this conversation a million times. Believe me, I know it doesn't pay to argue with him because he's always right. I especially didn't want to argue with him just then because I believed all I'd have to do was show him Lisa's picture and he'd understand. He's really pigheaded about abortion. He thinks it's murder when any sensible person knows that a baby, or whatever, isn't a human being until it's born. I really don't worry about it too much. Lots of my friends have taken their girlfriends to get abortions. In fact, even some gang members have done it. That's why I can't understand why Sandy's people were so pissed with me. After all, it was a decision made by _both_ of us, and she said she would make that clear to her family. But her brothers and their friends didn't seem to understand. I guess they were taking their Catholicism too seriously.

"Paul," I said finally, "would you get off your soapbox for just a minute and listen? It isn't like you haven't said his before. If you ever become a teacher, you will bore all your students by repeating yourself. Don't worry, I'm OK and don't plan to go back on any of my promises. With this girl, I don't even think of sex or anything nasty. You'll understand when you see her picture. Please do me _one_ favor and come into the foyer? We can talk later."

He was really reluctant, I could tell, but said he'd come with me. As we walked to the door, he said something about never being an idiot teacher because he'd be going to Harvard. Paul didn't know then that his early admission to Harvard would get rejected, and he'd be going to Stanford instead. At first he was really mad about it because some Harvard recruiter had come to school and told his AP English class Stanford was "the Harvard of the West Coast," but nobody would be dull enough to call Harvard "the Stanford of the East Coast." When he found out Stanford had better football and baseball teams, though, he was happy to go there instead of to Harvard.

Anyway, eventually we found ourselves in front of the trophy case. I showed him Lisa's picture, but he didn't seem impressed. He wanted to know who the dark girl on the other side was. He guessed wrongly that I knew because I already knew all the girls at school, even though classes hadn't started yet. My brother can really be a sarcastic son-of-a-bitch sometimes. I felt amazed but relieved that he didn't get all excited about Lisa and, despite his sarcasm, couldn't get mad at Paul that day. I really didn't know any girls at the high school yet, but was pleased with myself because, thanks to Coach Miller, I knew the name of the girl Paul was asking about.

Paul is not one to talk much about what he feels. I tell him everything, but he seldom tells me much in return. Sometimes it really irritates the hell out of me because I think it's a technique he uses to show me up. When I tell him something, he listens carefully. I know he hears what I say because later, when he's lecturing me about something, he can almost always repeat verbatim what I've told him. Since I am his older brother, he likes to have power over me. I've tried many times to be a good listener to him, especially when I know he's hurt or depressed. But he just clams up and won't tell me much until all I can do is try to get something out of him by asking a million questions. He will only give me the basic information, then refuse to tell me anything about his emotions or feelings.

On the day I'm talking about, I was so excited that I wanted to tell Paul all about Lisa. But all he did was stand there, looking at the picture of Lora. He didn't seem to even hear what I was saying. We walked home, and he listened to everything Coach Miller had said about the Hudsons. I told him everything because I know how tight-lipped Paul can be when he knows something about someone else's personal life. He said little on our way home, and after dinner I tried talking to him again, but he said he had lots to do and didn't want to be bothered anymore that night.

Then he shut the door of his room, and that was that. I wondered how Paul could be so insensitive when I was feeling so high. Perhaps his problem is that he's just not too deep.

Chapter Three

I had no idea how I would go about meeting Lisa. First, I thought I would just look around to see what I was dealing with. When school started, I began my surveillance. I got to school early to see if I could glimpse Lisa when she got there. As it turned out, she was hard to miss. After all, how many kids get transported to school in a chauffeur-driven limo? Sometimes parents just don't know what they do to their kids. If old Hudson wanted to make his daughters less conspicuous, he sure wasn't succeeding. Why didn't Alihandro just bring them to school in a Volkswagen or something? I almost felt embarrassed to be standing on the street corner *oohing* and *aahing* as Lisa and Lora got dropped off at school by their Nicaraguan chauffeur. But it was worth the embarrassment to see the girl of my dreams step out the back door when Alihandro opened it.

If anyone was with her, I didn't notice because the only person I saw stepping on the curb was my radiant beauty. I could go on and on about how striking she was, but I don't want to bore you. All I can say is that even her picture—the picture that inspired me to love her—didn't do her justice. I don't think I've ever seen anyone as beautiful.

Though I had trouble taking my eyes off her shimmering image, I was curious to see how other kids were reacting to the show taking place before them. There was lots of talking and joking going on as the limo drove up, but when Lisa stepped out and began walking toward the entrance, it all stopped and there was only silence. Most of the kids stared at her with an admiration almost bordering on reverence, if you can imagine that. Lisa walked by saying "Hi" to a few people out in front of the school. She didn't even look in my direction, and I was truly glad of that. For the first time since I started dressing differently, I felt ashamed of the way I must have looked standing there in spiked hair, earrings, black leather and chains.

I was looking at my boots when I felt Lisa go by with Lora in tow. By the time I looked up at the school's main entrance, Lisa had disappeared into it, but I still glimpsed Lora about to do the same. That's when I saw my brother watching her intently from nearby. Wow, I thought, Paul must have lost his cool.

I pondered that as I walked to my first class.

Later, there was a break of about 20 minutes between when the last class got dismissed and we had to suit up for football. They had canceled the pep squad practice that day, so I ran to the northwest corner of campus to see what I could see. Lisa and Lora were way ahead of me, already climbing into the limo. Alihandro closed the door behind them and drove off. I guess Miller was right about me getting with Lisa. For a long time I stood there watching the limo disappear, but then remembered that if I didn't get going, I'd be late for practice.

I remember feeling miserable for quite a few days. My classes were the same as always, boring as hell. You never get a better deal by going to a new school. And yet now school was the most exciting place to be because there was always the possibility of seeing Lisa. In fact, I saw her twice during passing periods, and always sat at a safe distance to watch her during lunch. She usually ate with her girlfriends. As far as I could tell, she didn't hang out with guys. I don't think she ever saw me, and I was glad of that, as I explained earlier, because I'm sure my appearance —and the fact that I was watching—would have put her off. She might even have thought I'm some kind of pervert. Judging from her looks, you'd never think I was her type at all; believe me, I really understood that.

Finally, I began putting together something of a plan. If I could just find out where she lived, maybe I could meet her. I remembered Miller telling me the Hudsons lived on an island where rich folks have their homes. There was only one place like that in the school district, and I was sure if I hung out there long enough, I'd discover Alihandro, the limo, or even the girls themselves.

As I walked over the bridge, though, I remembered what I was wearing. It occurred to me that, when the good people of this area saw me, they'd think I was a thief and call the cops or something. Then, about halfway over the bridge, I noticed a lowered black Cadillac following me down the street. For a second, I thought I recognized the car, and then, as it approached, I *knew* I did; there could be no mistake. The Cadillac passed slowly, allowing me to check out its driver. Just as I suspected, it was Boy Jerome, one of the biggest pimps and drug dealers on the city's west side where Paul and I used to live. We never called him "boy" to his face, of course; only Jerome or "sir" when he was within hearing distance. This guy meant business; we all knew that. And messing with him could cost you your life, I'm not kidding.

For a moment, I wondered what the hell he was doing in a nice place like this. Then again, I realized there was only one thing he *could* do, no matter *where* he was. It surprised me to learn that drugs were coming to a place like this, but it just confirms what you hear on the news. Drugs are everywhere. Now please, don't misunderstand me. Just because Jerome is Black and driving a Cadillac in a nice, pre-dominantly White neighborhood doesn't mean he's making a drug run. But I know enough about Boy Jerome to understand that this guy is so heavily into the drug world that he couldn't be doing anything else. You're going to have to trust me on this because I know what I'm talking about. Anyway, after he left, my fear of getting dragged off as a weirdo somewhat subsided, knowing that Jerome's presence must be something they were accustomed to here. I pretended I was just taking a walk, though really I was checking out the neighborhood.

The houses in this area are quite large, though the lots are small. Despite the postage-stamp lawns, though, there are gardeners crawling all over the place. And the flower beds look like those European gardens you see in travel magazines. Even though thick walls and well-built fences cut the backyards off from the gaze of passersby like me, I swear I just can't imagine there being enough back there to warrant all those gardeners. I call this a concrete island because it's surrounded by water. And not far away there's an enormous bay where my brother and I like to come to get some sun and watch the girls in their summer bikinis. All around the little island there are docks for yachts and other boats. I really felt happy walking along the canals, knowing that Lisa lived somewhere nearby. This would be a nice place to live if you had enough bucks and enjoyed living at a location resembling Disneyland.

I guess I hiked around for about half an hour before seeing Jerome's car scooting back across the bridge. Evidently, he'd completed his transaction. As I walked further down the same street I'd walked down before, I noticed a garage door open that earlier had been closed.

Suddenly, a Hispanic-looking woman entered from its rear door and started closing the main door in front. Then, as the opening got smaller, I glimpsed the limo I'd hoped I'd see. Walking home, I said to myself, "So this is where Lisa lives!" And I remember thinking, "How can I ever get close to a girl like that?"

I had completed my mission and found out what I needed to know. I hurried on home before something happened. Crossing the bridge, I thought I noticed a couple of funny looks from people along the street, but perhaps it was just my imagination.

I really agonized about what to do next, and it took me a few days to decide. You probably think I was neglecting everything, focusing so much on this girl. But it was really otherwise. I know you'll think I'm a nut or some corny uncool jerk, but I really wanted to be worthy of Lisa. I couldn't help thinking about the days of knights and armor when men did all they could to make themselves look good in the eyes of the women they loved. These knights thought of themselves as contemptible, so when their ladies even glanced their way, they felt like they'd received the greatest gift in the world. And here I was, acting just like them. In other ways, though, I was nothing like them at all. I couldn't really call myself a knight because I really was just a low-class creep. Look at me! I had no money, dressed like some kind of hoodlum, got lousy grades, and had no apparent future.

But then I'd seen Lisa, and suddenly everything started making sense. Like the knights in the stories, I loved my lady from afar. She inspired me to try for better grades. After all, she was an excellent student herself. Football practice was not the drag that it used to be, and I looked forward to doing "heroic deeds" on the football field. Which was about the closest thing to a battlefield I can imagine in high school.

I kept thinking if I could do something startling enough on the football field, Lisa couldn't help but notice. The way I dress wouldn't matter then because I'd be in a football uniform. I even tried my hand at writing a few poems, but I'm really a lousy poet, and would be too embarrassed to let you read anything I wrote. In fact, I'd better stop talking like this or you'll think I'm a creep and put down this book. That would be too bad because you'd miss a pretty interesting story, if I say so myself.

Anyway, I hung around Lisa's house on the weekends to see what might come up. I had to do something about the way I looked, so I dressed like one of the many gardeners that haunt this little island on which my lady lives. Even though it was hot, I wore an army coat and covered up my spikes. I bought a fake mustache at a costume shop and stuck it on my lip under my nose. I put on blue jeans and didn't bother taking off my army boots because some gardeners wore boots just like them.

About a week later, I got my chance. I was taking a stroll down Lisa's street when I noticed the Hispanic woman I'd seen earlier making her way along the sidewalk on the other side loaded down with two full-to-the-brim shopping bags while trying to control two small children. They were about a block away from Lisa's house when one kid, a little girl about three, broke away from her mom and started running in the direction of the house. She ran towards the street, and I could see that she was about to cross it without stopping or looking in either direction. A car was coming, and any fool could see that it would definitely hit that little girl. The mother shouted loudly in Spanish for her to stop, but she kept right on running. Fortunately, I was close enough to run out and grab her just before she would have been hit. I jerked her out of its path in the nick of time. Within seconds, the mother was at my side, thanking me profusely in Spanish. I know a little Spanish, so it wasn't hard to catch the drift of what she was saying. She must have thanked me a hundred times. I felt embarrassed by all her loud gratitude and didn't want to call too much attention to myself.

"Let me help you with your groceries," I offered.

I took both sacks, and she didn't argue because of what had almost just happened. She thanked me again, took the hands of her two children firmly in her own and started off towards Lisa's house. The little girl complained that her mother was holding her hand too tight, but the mother told her in Spanish that she'd better be quiet and if she ever tried breaking away like that again, she'd have a very sore little butt (the word is difficult to translate) and a squeezed hand would be the least of her worries.

The mother and I didn't have much time to talk because we were quickly reaching our destination. I was thinking I'd take the grocery sacks up to the front porch and be on my merry way when she asked my name and what I did for a living.

"I'm Manuel Ortega," I told her, "and someday I want to be a gardener. For now, though, I'm still in high school." I don't know why, but those were the first words that popped into my head. As far as I know, I had never heard that name before.

"Well," she said, pointing towards the house, "my husband is the gardener and driver here. He's been doing lots of driving lately and could use some part-time help. Would you be interested in working in the garden on weekends?

I could hardly control my excitement. This would be the perfect way to see Lisa and perhaps even speak to her now and then!

"Sure," I said.

She said her name was Maria and asked whether I'd be kind enough to help carry the groceries through the garage to the servant's entrance in back. Then she pulled the automatic garage door opener out of her purse, opened the garage door, and off we went. In the backyard, Maria instructed me to wait while she took everything, including the children, inside.

"Mr. Hudson, the owner, is home," she said. "I'll speak to him about the part-time gardening job."

While she was gone, I wondered why a house with such a small yard needed two gardeners. Maybe the border patrol had caught Alihandro, and I would be his replacement. I just didn't know. I also remembered I was still wearing earrings. Hopefully, my blue-knit ski cap was down low enough, so she hadn't noticed them. I didn't want these people to think I was some kind of maniac, get scared, and send me away. Feeling kind of worried, I pulled out the studs as fast as I could and placed them in my pockets. Then I started worrying about the holes in my ears, so I pulled the ski cap down over my ears even further to make sure they weren't visible. Suddenly the door popped open, and an old man seemed to jump out at me. It was obviously Mr. Hudson. He was gushing and slobbering and patting me on the back like I was his best friend or something. I could tell he'd been drinking because I smelled alcohol on his breath, but he must have also been drinking garlic because the odor coming from his mouth was the worst I've ever smelled. Geese, I wondered, why wasn't he wearing a mask?

For a minute I pitied Mrs. Hudson and wondered what she did when her husband smelled like that. Then I remembered what Coach Miller had said about her wandering ways. I had little time to think, though, because suddenly Hudson seemed to be all over me. Maria stood in the doorway trying to tell me in Spanish that this was Mr. Hudson, but I had already drawn that conclusion, as I have told you. I wondered how his breath could stink so much and how he could start drinking so early in the morning. It was only 10 a.m. for Chrissake!

"Congratulations on saving that child!" Hudson was saying. For a moment, I felt a warm glow inside because I'd never saved a life before and it had just happened 15 minutes earlier. "You're a good boy. Maria tells me you're looking for a job."

He said he needed a part-time gardener to help, and weekend work would be fine. "Do you have a green card?" the old man wanted to know. I guess he assumed I was just off the boat because Maria was talking to me in Spanish.

I told him I was born in the US, though my parents came from Mexico, which was true, and that I went to high school and had a social security number and all that. Hudson seemed relieved. "That's great, son," he said. "Then there won't be any problem at all." I guess he was thinking about Alihandro's uncertain status with immigration. "What do you say I pay you a few bucks under the table?" he asked. "What if I give you $15 an hour and we just won't worry about social security, worker's comp and all that, OK? You'll be really careful and not get hurt, won't you? This house is just a single story, and Alihandro has kept the trees down, so you won't have to get up too high."

I thought $15 an hour wasn't much, but at least I wouldn't have to pay taxes on it. And then I remembered why I was in his backyard to begin with, and it sure wasn't to make any money.

"Thank you very much, sir," I said, "all that sounds fine." I tried to be as polite as possible, though I really felt turned off by Mr. Hudson.

The old man was offering me the deal of a lifetime and didn't even know it.

"There's just one thing, son," he said. "Can you fill out this job application for me? It's a backyard special that one of my daughters typed up. It's only a formality that gives me some basic information, so I can call you at home or contact your parents if anything comes up. Maria, will you get the form for me? It's in the top drawer on the right-hand side of my desk in the study."

Maria left immediately, and suddenly I experienced a moment of panic. Would Hudson ask for references and call around about me? Would he call up my dad and blow the whole thing? I felt myself breaking into a cold sweat.

Maria reappeared an instant later with the paper. And then Hudson said, "Don't worry about anything, son," as if he could sense my nervousness. "I just need some basic information for my own personal needs. I won't make a federal case out of this because it's just a part-time weekend job and we're going to keep our pay agreement secret, if that's all right with you."

That made me feel a little better, but as I took the form from him, I wondered how I was going to fill it out. I'm a pretty good liar, as you have probably gathered by now, but that doesn't mean I feel *comfortable* about lying. And with guys like Hudson, you never know exactly what you're getting into.

Hudson told me he'd really be glad to have me around. He was one of those guys who doesn't know how to keep his distance and comes right up to your face to talk. I could smell his bad breath again. He must have patted me on the back 50 times and said what a hero I was for what I'd done for Maria and for him too, because he loved Maria's children just like he loved his own. He told me I could fill the paper out around the back of the house. His daughters were out there with a couple of friends, he said, but they wouldn't bother me. When I finished the application, I could just give it to Maria, and she would have Alihandro show me around. If I wanted to start right away, he said, I could. Or I could start work on Sunday. He didn't care. Or I could even take the weekend off and start next Saturday, if that's what I wanted.

I thanked Hudson as politely as I could and was glad to see him go back into the house. His odor seemed to linger in the air. Old guys like him, and middle-aged people really get me. I just don't see that there's any point to their lives. It's as if they only had a brief time to be with it in high school, or maybe even college, and then spend the rest of their lives being caretakers to younger people.

Like my dad, all he does is work. What fun can it be? I don't think he's as out-of-it as some other older people I see around. But I guess that's because he's my dad. I know other kids think my dad's a turkey because he doesn't seem to care how he looks or dresses and does nothing interesting or exciting. I mean, he's lucky enough to live down by the beach and all, but he doesn't even ever go there. He says he already has a tan and that burning yourself to a crisp is dangerous. He reads the newspaper avidly and says they're just now seeing how much damage the sun does to your skin.

Going to the store is about the only time he ever leaves the house. And going to work, of course. He keeps the apartment clean and doesn't expect my brother and me to do anything but take care of our own rooms. When he's not cleaning or cooking or going to the store, he's usually watching sports on TV. He drinks beer, but never over two. I have never seen him drunk. He has a job where he only gets a week off every year, and all he does then is watch sports on TV and drink two beers a day. He doesn't go out with girls a lot. He says he's trying to save money for our college educations. I don't know why he's doing that, because Paul's scholarship will pay for his, and I'm not even going. When I tell him this, he tells me I'll change my mind. After all, he tells me, I have the potential to go to college.

He goes out with one girl he knows about once a month, and sometimes he doesn't even come home on these nights. He's been doing this for a couple of years, and I can't understand how either he or his girlfriend can live like that. He doesn't even like to take drives unless he goes to visit my mother's grave at Forest Lawn, which happens once a week on Sunday. He says he doesn't really need to drive anywhere anyway. After all, he says, he lives at the beach.

These thoughts about my father are what's coming to me right now. I don't think I was thinking about Dad standing in Hudson's backyard wondering what I was going to do with the form he gave me. I know I thought briefly how out-of-it Hudson was. After all, he had enough money to show some class with his personal appearance, and he could've done something about how bad he smelled. But it seemed these rich guys are even worse than other people because they look stupid and act stupid just like everybody else, but really could do something about it if they wanted.

Hudson said his daughters were around the back of the house. I felt all excited, like I usually do when I plan on seeing Lisa. But now that I'd be seeing her in her own backyard, I got scared again. I mean, I wasn't exactly presentable in the disguise I was wearing and wondered what kind of impression I'd make, or if she'd even notice me at all.

As I rounded the corner of the house, I saw the backyard was more spacious than I'd imagined. I don't mean it was huge, but there was sure enough space to be comfortable. There was a very nice patio area near the back of the house, and things seemed pretty well landscaped except for the flower beds that got torn up when they put the new wall in. There were four girls sitting at a picnic table under an awning talking to each other. Lisa and Lora were there with another girl I knew was on the pep squad.

The fourth girl was rather large-looking and maybe even fat. She had obviously not taken much pain in dressing, wearing a long skirt or dress or something. She didn't really attract my interest, so I didn't look at her much. The other girls wore shorts and tank tops and sandals. And all of their faces were covered by the dumb masks everyone has to wear these days to keep from getting some stupid virus. I was wearing one too. And, as it was still early September and pretty hot outside, I was burning up in my army jacket wishing I had on shorts and sandals like them.

There was another picnic table on the lawn near enough to just make out what the girls were saying. They didn't seem to notice when I sat down at it and acted like I was busy filling out the form. They were speaking in low tones, like what they were talking about was some kind of big secret, but I could still hear them.

The pep-squad girl, whose name I didn't know, was holding a newspaper. She was reading the story about the game the night before to the other three girls. Lisa and Lora had lots to say in response to the story, but the heavy-looking girl said very little..

Lora commented that the game on Friday night was the most exciting she'd ever seen. She was surely glad the Santos brothers were on the team, because they scored a couple of touchdowns that really made a difference in the outcome.

I couldn't believe what she was reading. Hearing the name "Santos" surprised me. That I was listening to a conversation like this excited me, and I tried even harder to tune into what they were saying.

Lora was saying she'd seen Paul Santos at school, and he was good-looking but seemed snobbish, just like all the other handsome jocks they'd ever known.

"Still, Lora," the nameless pepster in shorts said, "if he asked you out, you'd probably go with him, wouldn't you?"

"Sure I would, Stephanie," Lora said. "His good looks would be interesting, even if he was the greatest snob in the world. But you seem to forget one thing; Daddy dear is a nut who keeps me and my sister locked up like prisoners in our own house. If it wasn't for streaming TV, I'd be climbing the walls every day."

She paused.

"It's not so bad for Lisa," she said, glancing at her sister. "She's an outstanding student who wants to go to Radcliffe or someplace like that. She's always studying her butt off, anyway. Besides, I hear Paul is some kind of boring egghead who wants to go to some super college like Lisa does."

"But don't you think Paul's just about the best-looking guy at school?" Stephanie wanted to know..

"I agree with you, Stephanie," Lora said, "but what good does that do me or my sister? He's a big junior and would probably never think of dating a sophomore. And besides, before long, he'll be taking out Mary or Rachael or some other sexy junior or senior on the pep squad. If you're really interested, Stephanie, why don't you just go up to him and introduce yourself? Your parents don't put any strings on you. You're free to do as you please and, remember, as a liberated junior, you can ask out any guy you want."

Stephanie blushed but didn't respond. The big girl just sat there in silence.

"I don't know why you two are so hung up on Paul Santos," Lisa said. "I really don't get what you see in him. He has a pretty face, but that's about all. I bet he's plastic as hell and would bore you to death. What does he do but hurry around the halls with his nose in the air and play football? I hear he's a brain and has early admission to Stanford. But isn't this all just a little silly?"

Lora seemed to bristle. "I can't believe what you're saying, Lisa," she said. "You and Paul are the same. He's just a little further down the road than you are. Are you jealous or something? Are you bothered that he's a snob and doesn't pay attention to you like everybody else does? I think Stephanie and I have finally got your number."

"No," Lisa said, "that's where you're wrong. I look for character in a man. Paul Santos doesn't interest me at all. If I had to choose between the Santos brothers, I'd pick Michael in a heartbeat."

I couldn't believe what I was hearing! I almost fell over backwards off the picnic bench. Was I dreaming or something? I don't know what I was thinking, but I looked at the paper I was filling out and noticed that I hadn't written a word.

When I could finally concentrate again, I heard Lora and Stephanie telling Lisa what a creep I was. Had she seen how I dressed? I probably didn't even take a shower after football practice, and I was probably a homicidal maniac and so on. Lora asked the heavy girl if she didn't agree that Michael Santos was a creep, and she said, "He sure is!" in a low and husky voice. Apparently her name was Paula, and she seemed to look in my direction when she confirmed what a creep Michael Santos was. When I saw she was looking at me, I lowered my eyes and pretended to be working on the paper. I was beginning to understand why I never found Lora attractive, and I was disliking those other two girls as well.

"I know all I hear from you two is Paul Santos," Lisa went on. "But Michael, to me, is the more interesting creature. He's a weird dresser, but I like that. He seems to be a loner and doesn't really need to take his identity from a crowd of other people. A good football player is what he is. I've seen no one, even the pros, who can elude the backfield and catch a football like he can. I've heard all kinds of things about him; that he's intelligent and doesn't need to get good grades to prove it. I hear he works at the beauty salon a couple hours a day as a part of the R.O.P. class he's in. Some girls say he really does a marvelous job on their hair. You know, I admire Michael because he seems to have the courage to do some things I'm afraid to do. And he's not bad looking at all if you can just see through all those black clothes and weird hairdos and earrings and leather boots."

I'm really embarrassed about this now. I know I didn't tell you I work at a beauty salon every day before football practice. This isn't exactly something I brag about, if you know what I mean. A few of the guys on the team know about it and rib me sometimes. I'm sensitive about their little innuendos, suggesting that I'm a fag or something. I keep telling them to check out an old movie my dad turned me onto called *Shampoo*, but they never do, and no one seems to have ever seen it but me. Anyway, it's about this handsome guy played by an actor named Warren Beatty, who's a hairdresser. Everyone thinks he's gay, but he isn't. In fact, he goes out with his clients and makes love to them all, and one of them is an actress named Goldie Hawn, who is cute. He's got more women in his life than he knows what to do with.

This is really not the time to tell you this, but since I'm hanging out all my dirty laundry in this story, I may as well tell you everything. You know there's really only one thing in the world that I fear more than death, and that's being a fag. I'd rather kill myself than be gay, in fact. But how does someone know when he's homosexual, if you know what I mean? I hear there are more queers and lesbians out there than anyone can imagine. I've heard that you can go through most of your life making love to girls and women and loving them up with the best. You can even have a wife and family and be a respectable citizen with a good job and lots of money, and then you just get up one morning and look at yourself in the mirror when you're shaving and say to yourself, "I'm a flaming faggot!" I hear this can happen to you, especially when you're over 40.

Just thinking about this makes me sick to my stomach. If someone came up to me and said, "Would you rather live as a queer or have me run you over with a Mack truck?" I'd say without even thinking about it, "Bring on the truck, mister!" But I don't think it's really a matter of choice. Can you imagine anyone choosing to be homosexual? Please don't get the wrong idea, I'm really not against gay people. I know how creative they can be. I know that they're superb people and all that. In fact, I'm not a bigot about anybody. Not about Anglos or Blacks or even about some of my people who act like a bunch of horses' asses sometimes. I don't have the slightest impulse to make fun of somebody because he's gay or go out and beat up queers or anything like that. To tell the truth, though, that worries me a bit. Why am I so sympathetic to gays if I'm not one myself? I don't think there's any end to worrying about things like this, so I'll drop it to keep from boring you and just tell you what's important.

I didn't get into the R.O. P Cosmetology Program because I was interested in it. To tell you the truth, I was in danger of flunking out of school. I've told you before that I'm not very good at studying and that I'm stupid or something and don't get good grades. I heard that R.O.P. offered Mickey Mouse classes that anybody could pass, and besides, you could get out of school for part of the day and even maybe make some money at it. I went down to talk to the people at my old high school, and I picked cosmetology as a kind of joke. If I was going to do something weird, why not go all the way? To make a long story short, I found the training interesting and seem to have a flair for working on hair. In fact, some girls on the pep squad skip school to come down to the salon and have me work on them. It's a great way to meet chicks, and I used to use my job for that until I saw Lisa.

Anyway, I was sitting at the picnic bench dumbfounded, not hearing what the girls were saying anymore, when I noticed two people standing behind me and looking over my shoulder. It was Maria and Alihandro. I guess it was time for my tour of the yard. Maria introduced me to Alihandro, her husband, and as I told you earlier, I'd seen him many times, although this was the first time I'd actually *met* him. Maria went back to the house, leaving me with her husband. He smiled and thanked me in Spanish for rescuing his daughter. Then he began leading me around the yard. I remember little of what he told me because I was thinking about what I'd heard the girls saying. One thing I remember, though, is him telling me that the yard was small, but Mr. Hudson was constantly redoing the landscaping and moving the plants around. And when that was done, there was always plenty of painting to do because Hudson liked everything looking spit and polished.

When we came around the side of the house and approached the patio area, I noticed that some sort of uproar was taking place over where the girls had been talking. Everyone was on her feet screaming, and Lisa and Stephanie broke off and ran into the house, while Lora actually looked like she was fainting. I saw her go limp and fall down on the grass, dead weight. I know she wasn't faking because no one could fall down like that and be pretending. If she'd hit her head on a rock, she'd have killed herself.

As I came closer to where Paula was still standing, I could see that somehow a rattlesnake had gotten into the yard. I wondered how a snake could have crawled over the bridge without getting run over by a car, and then it occurred to me it was probably someone's pet that had escaped from its cage. The snake was all coiled up, its tail rattling, and striking at Paula, who didn't really seem afraid at all. I didn't know what to do because I've always had a fear of snakes. So I turned my head to look at Alihandro and saw he was nowhere to be found. While I was dicking around, not knowing what to do, Paula picked up a hockey stick lying in the grass and lunged at the snake, killing it with a knock over the head just as clean as a whistle.

Immediately, she hurried over to me and handed me the stick. "Listen, Mike," she said in a low whisper, "as far as anyone knows, *you* did this, ok? Just keep your mouth shut and I'll explain everything later."

There was something strange about that voice. It was too deep for a girl's and weirdly familiar. Was she a transgender? Did she have a penis? I've heard that some boys dress up like girls and then get their dicks cut off. Thinking about that almost makes me throw up, so I try not to think of it too much. But now I was staring at this girl, wondering if she was really a guy with a penis, and suddenly she pulled down her mask and almost made me faint.

It wasn't a girl at all, but my brother Paul, dressed up in drag! I couldn't believe what I was seeing. I've always had my doubts about Paul, as I've told you before, but this was really too much. Was my brother secretly a transgender? And if he was, what in the heck did that make me? It seemed like this day would never end with its shocks and surprises. I stood there dumbly holding the hockey stick in both hands, not knowing what to do, as he pulled the mask back up over his mouth and nose. Although I fear snakes, I had come up with some kind of plan to help the girls, but now I couldn't even remember what it was. All I could do was look at the dead snake, then at my brother, and then back at the snake again.

In a minute, Hudson—the only one in that yard *without* a mask— was at my elbow thanking me, patting me on the back, and breathing on me. This time, I thought I really *was* going to throw up because I was so confused and upset. And as all this was going on, Alihandro danced up to the group while "Paula," pulling "her" mask down once again, performed mouth-to-mouth on Lora to revive her. It wasn't too hard to imagine what _else_ my brother was getting out of it. Then Alihandro started singing a song in Spanish about heroic combat and knights in armor and all. I thought this was an obvious effort to cover up his cowardice, but no one seemed to pay attention.

Through all the confusion I seem to remember Hudson saying I had put in a good day of work already and could take Sunday off. Before I knew it, the man of the house was escorting me through the garage and then we were standing on the sidewalk in front of the house. I know he thanked me about a thousand times more and said he'd see me the following Sunday. The truth, though, is that I saw little of Hudson after that. From then on, I mainly dealt with Maria, and believed Hudson had forgotten about pretty much everything that happened that day.

I remember walking home as if I were moving in a dream. When I got there, I noticed someone had cleaned the house and my father sat watching a baseball game on TV. I said nothing to him but went directly to the refrigerator for a beer. Though my father's liquor was strictly off limits, on this day I didn't care. I really needed a beer. If Dad caught me, well, I'd just have to suffer the consequences. I took one of his drinks, hid it under my coat, and went to my room to wait for my brother. My dad didn't miss his beer and, if he did, he said nothing about it.

Chapter Four

When I got to my room, I tried relaxing as best as I could. I imagined sipping at the beer slowly to get a high off just that one can, but ended up chugging it down, finishing in about a minute. I still felt like the day had mixed me up in a weird dream with a mysterious outcome I could not yet discern. Though I was excited, I also felt worried and afraid. I couldn't imagine what my brother was doing in that backyard dressed like a girl. Clearly, I lacked enough information to take any action just yet. So I sat on my hands, waiting to talk to him. I wished he'd hurry and get home! The idea of sitting on my hands put a thought in my head. I've heard that smokers smoke because they don't know what to do with their hands. So it occurred to me that maybe I could use a smoke. I started looking around my room for the pack of cigarettes I'd hidden in various places so Dad or my brother wouldn't find it. The trouble was that I'd forgotten where I'd last hidden it, so I had to spend 10 minutes looking everywhere. Actually, I was glad to have something to do, happy to pass the time until Paul got home.

When I finally found the cigarettes, I grabbed one and put the pack back in a different hiding place. I don't know why I'm always hiding my cigarettes in different places because, no matter where I hide them, someone could find them by accidentally looking in the right place. I guess I just like to be secretive and have a life of my own.

And the more of a big deal I can make of it, the better I feel about my cleverness, or something like that. I don't think a cigarette now and then will hurt you, though I've heard in school that even breathing smoke from someone else's cigarettes can be deadly. I've seen those sickening advertisements where they cut out someone's lung who's died of lung cancer, and the inside of it looks like burned meat. I don't know why I smoke at all; I don't even really like it. But occasionally I feel the need for it as I did right then, so I keep at least one pack on hand. But, like I said, I try to keep them well hidden because I'm afraid if Paul found them or caught me smoking, he'd turn me into the coach. He's such a Puritan, as I told you before, and you can never really depend on people like that, especially when you're doing something they think is wrong. And there's no doubt Paul thinks smoking is bad for everyone, but especially for athletes and kids. I don't think he'd let himself get caught dead with a cigarette in his mouth.

I used to smoke quite a lot when I was in junior high school. That was before I really got involved in sports. My dad did everything he could to stop me, but he really couldn't do very much. We finally made peace about it, and I agreed not to smoke in my room or the apartment or in any public place where an adult could see me. The yard was the best place for me to smoke, but when I found out my dad would let me do it, smoking sort of lost its appeal. He and I haven't talked about it in a long time, though I imagine the same rules hold. I knew I was breaking the rules by smoking in my room, but this was the weirdest day in my life, and I didn't care. I'd noticed coming in that the game my dad was watching was still in its early innings, so I didn't think he'd come bugging me soon. By then, the aroma of smoke would likely be gone. Paul, though, could come home any minute. "Oh hell," I told myself, "stop worrying and try to calm down!"

When I finished the cigarette, I realized my room was kind of messy and killed a little time cleaning it up. I made my bed and picked up my clothes and straightened up some of the crap on the bookshelves. My homework was lying in disorder all over the desk, but I knew there was a kind of order in the disorder and figured I'd better leave that mess alone for now. I glanced at my watch and noticed I'd only been there for half an hour. So I got the vacuum out to clean the carpet, and when I finished, went back to the kitchen and mixed up a batch of vinegar and water to wash the windows from inside.

Walking by the den, I could see my father still watching the baseball game. He was drinking a beer. That made me want another one, but I didn't dare take it out of the refrigerator. I don't understand how Dad can just sit in a dark room watching TV. He loves a dark house, I guess, because he always draws the curtains closed whenever he's at home. When he's gone, I go around and pull all the window coverings open again because I like sunshine and fresh air. I sure am glad I have my room so I can let in as much light and air as I want.

After I'd finished washing the windows, I went to Paul's room and picked up one of his sports magazines. Then I returned to my room, stretched out on the bed, and started reading an article. I felt better already because I'd had my beer and cigarettes and, besides, having the room clean always makes me feel good anyway, though I would never admit that to anyone. On this weird Saturday, it was probably cleaner than it had ever been. I usually sort of let it get filthy over a couple of weeks, then suddenly decide to super clean it like I did on that Saturday.

Anyway, the article I was reading was about a 21-year-old guy who loved climbing up the face of steep cliffs like El Capitan in Yosemite National Park and places like that. One day he and a friend got caught in a snowstorm, and for a long time no one could find them. After the rangers rescued them, they discovered that the first guy was so badly frostbitten that they had to cut off both his legs at the knees. He felt bad about losing his legs, but even worse because one of the rescuers had died. I guess he fell out of a helicopter or something. Don't ask me what happened to the guy's buddy because I don't remember. After all, I read this article several months ago and I don't have the best memory in the world or anything like that. I think his friend was all right, though. Anyway, this guy who lost his legs got some fake ones for himself so he could keep climbing. The magazine had a picture of them. They had little plastic cups or something on one end of two pieces of metal that looked like pipes. The cups had straps on them so the guy could keep them on his stumps. He also had other fake legs to use when he wasn't climbing.

But the thing I found most interesting was that, on the foot-end of the little pipe legs he used for climbing, were two wooden feet that looked more like goat's hoofs than feet. There were three pictures of him climbing El Capitan, or somewhere, with his pipe legs and goat's feet on, and I couldn't help laughing. I really admired this guy and all but laughed anyway. This made me feel really guilty. It seemed like this guy used his arms mostly anyway, and he was a skinny guy, but you could see that his arms were really muscular and strong. I could just see him attached to a rope swinging around on some steep cliff wearing his pipe legs with goat's feet, and I had to laugh. I don't know what's the matter with me. I felt so guilty that I stopped reading the article and noticed that only 20 minutes had gone by.

Then I tried going to my desk to do homework. Maybe if I could get involved in some kind of thinking process, the time would pass faster. I worked on math but, as usual, couldn't get interested, especially just then. I kept trying to focus on the problems, but just couldn't. My mind kept going to a problem that seemed so much more important, namely how had Lisa noticed me without my knowing and what was my brother doing dressed as a girl? Every chance I get at school, I go to where Lisa is and check her out. I can't keep my eyes off of her, as you already know, and yet I never see her look at me or even in my direction.

This is something about females I'll never understand. They are so subtle that you never know what they're up to. Not too long ago when we were moving from our old neighborhood, a friend came over and told me it was too bad I was leaving because this chick I'd liked for a long time actually liked me back, even though I'd never seen her so much as glance at me. Turns out she was just acting coy. That really excited me. You get kind of jazzed when you find out a girl you've been drooling over really likes you, too. I wonder why girls act like that, why some play so hard-to-get? It just makes no sense. This friend who came over made me feel bad about leaving, but I wish he hadn't even come over because I'd really given up on the girl and had almost forgotten her. And now I was getting all excited again but couldn't do anything about it because I was leaving. And I'll be damned if I ever go back to that neighborhood because now I have other things to think about and do.

Since I couldn't keep my mind on my homework, I made dinner. Though I'm not a splendid cook, I can do a couple of simple things like spaghetti. Which makes me proud that I'll never starve if I find myself in a kitchen with food in the refrigerator. Everything I needed to make spaghetti was right there. We even had some French bread, so I thought I'd make that cheese bread that Dad and Paul like so much. When I passed by the den, I noticed the game was in the eighth inning, and figured Dad would be ready to eat pretty soon. I hoped Paul would walk in the door pretty quickly too. It took me about half an hour to get everything ready. The game ended and Dad came into the kitchen, but Paul still wasn't there. Dad was pleased as hell that I'd fixed dinner because I knew he really didn't get off on cooking too much, though he did about 90 percent of the cooking at our place. He said he was starving and asked if I'd mind him sampling some of the spaghetti and a piece of bread. Dad reminded me it was only four o'clock, and he hoped Paul would get home soon. I knew then that I'd really screwed up. We normally eat around five, and Paul might not walk in for another hour. By then, the spaghetti would be all sticky and the bread hard. I almost started crying because I felt so frustrated and sorry for myself.

Sure enough, about an hour later, Paul walked in. He didn't look like a girl anymore, and he seemed all fresh and happy. That was unusual for Paul. I wondered what was going on. Dad wasn't around when Paul walked in, so he came up to me and said, "Hey, Mike, I'm really sorry about what happened today. I know I owe you an explanation. So why don't we get together and take a walk to the beach, and I'll explain what's going on and maybe you can tell me what you're up to too."

I told him that was a good idea, and we'd talk later.

We never really talk much at the dinner table as a family, and this night was no exception. Dad complimented me twice on the bread and spaghetti, but I knew it didn't really taste that good. Besides, I think Paul and I were so eager to talk things out that neither of us cared much about what we were eating.

After we'd finished, Paul announced our plans to walk down to the beach and Dad said he'd do the dishes. On the way there, my brother just talked and talked. I'd never seen him go on like that about anything. He's not a naturally talkative guy, as I told you before, unless you've done something wrong and he's lecturing you about it. But he rarely talks much about himself. On our walk, though, he seemed all excited. He talked all fast and ran his sentences together and stuff, when usually he talks slow, pronouncing everything correctly and never muddling his thoughts. "Wow, I'm really smitten with that girl, Lora," he said. That's a word no one uses but Paul, *smitten.*

"What the heck does that mean?" I asked.

"It means I've found the girl of my dreams," he said, and we were off to the races.

He was so hung up on her, Paul said, that he didn't know what to do with himself. He described her in great detail and told me all about her likes and dislikes and what she talks about and all. This guy was obviously lovesick, and I felt sorry for him because I knew what he was going through. But it surprised me how he seemed to notice all the details about this chick when I really thought she was just ordinary. But gradually I realized that, during the past couple of weeks, Paul's love affair had caught him in its snare just as much as mine had caught me up in its own trap. To be honest, I hadn't noticed what was happening to Paul because I couldn't have cared less. And even now he was boring me, and I wished he'd get to the part I wanted to know about. Like why he had dressed as a girl. I mean, how could this guy go on and on about an ordinary chick like Lora?

We were walking along the bay now, just approaching a place called "Horny Corner." I don't know why, but I'm embarrassed to tell you the name of this place because of what you might think. I don't know when it got its name or who named it, and I'm not exactly sure why it's called "Horny Corner." All I can do is tell you what goes on there. As Paul and I approached the place, it was already almost dark, and the beach looked deserted. But during the summer, this patch of sand at the bay is so crowded that you can hardly find a spot, especially at its center. I mean, believe me, the sunbathers almost lie on top of each other. If you tried to park yourself there after 10 a.m. you'd be lucky to find a place to spread your towel. I don't know when these people actually get there to find their places because the same people seem to be there day after day, as if they never leave. Obviously they leave sometime, though, because here we were on a September evening and the place looked completely deserted.

Anyway, Horny Corner is the place for the beautiful people. I guess you could say it's like an outdoor singles bar, if you know what I mean. The people there get very dark in the summer. Heck, I've been there in June and they're black as ebony then too. They're not actually Black, though, but mostly Anglo. That's not to say there aren't any Blacks or Mexicans or whatever around because there are always some sitting on the cement wall, or playing basketball on the courts nearby, or lying out on the edge of Horny Corner. But they're never in the center, that's for sure.

I only go down there once in a while in summer because I really don't know what to think of the place. I mean, when you're there, you think you're on a Hollywood set for some sophisticated beach movie, if you know what I mean. I don't exactly fit in there. First, I'm not sure how old the people are. I don't think they're high school kids because I don't recognize any of them. The high school kids usually either hang out at the pier or on the peninsula or at some other place at the bay. Horny Corner isn't exactly for high school kids, as far as I can tell. My brother is good-looking enough to get near the center of Horny Corner, but we've talked about it before, and he really feels no more comfortable there than I do. I'm not sure, but it seems they reserve Horny Corner for college kids and maybe not even *them* when I think about it. Maybe these people are already out of college. I really don't know. There is a mystery at the center of Horny Corner that I don't think I'll ever crack.

All I know is that the people there are really beautiful—I mean *really* beautiful. You've got to believe me about that. And they seem to know how to talk to each other because they talk and laugh like crazy. They circulate a lot. The chicks move little, but the guys move from towel to towel, talking to the girls. I don't know how these guys do it, but the girls never seem bored or scornful or whatever and even talk and laugh with the guys a lot too. It's like they're all part of one great big social group where everyone really likes and admires everyone else and has a good time talking and joking with each other. These people never bring silly things to the beach like beach balls and floats or whatever. You see no children at the center of Horny Corner, though they are down by the water and playing in the sand everywhere else. But you get the idea the people really "with it" at Horny Corner would never bring kids to the beach.

In fact, it would surprise me if any of them even have kids.

There's not supposed to be any booze on the beach, but the people at the Corner's center regularly bring their hooch in all kinds of containers, cleverly hiding the fact that they're sucking up alcohol like crazy. If the cops know about this, they apparently don't care because I've seen nobody get busted for drinking at Horny Corner, though I've seen people get hassled at other places at the Bay or along the beach. I know the cops like to go to Horny Corner because they're always around yet bother no one. Whenever they can strike up a conversation, they do and seem to enjoy the scenery as much as anyone else. Some cops look pretty good in their summer uniforms, wearing shorts and short-sleeved shirts. I saw a really nice-looking lady cop in some tight-fitting shorts last summer. I don't want to get too involved in this, but I will tell you I really go wild about a girl in a uniform of any kind. I'm not sure why; maybe someday I'll ask a psychiatrist.

Well, anyway, occasionally the people at Horny Corner get pretty rambunctious. I've even seen some guys gang up on girls and throw them in the water. The funny thing about it, though, is that nobody ever gets their hair wet. Even when a girl gets thrown in, somehow her head stays above water. Usually the girls don't even cool themselves in the water but prefer to squirt their bodies with little bottles like window washers use.

I hope I'm not boring you with everything I'm saying about the Corner, but I'll be damned if I'm going to tell you what my brother was saying about Lora on our way down to the beach because that would bore you even more.

Paul and I don't go to the Corner very much because we don't exactly fit in, as I was telling you earlier. But sometimes we lay out our towels near where we can check things out and look at the chicks, trying to figure out what's going on. Both of us believe that if we could move in closer to the center, we'd learn something really valuable that would probably help us later in life. Sometimes I go down there alone because Paul is busy with something or another and doesn't hang out at the beach as much as I do.

One day I was there by myself and noticed this fantastic-looking girl leaning against a backrest, reading a book. She wasn't at the center of things, but she was pretty close to it. I noticed no one was bugging her, and sort of checked her out for half an hour. It surprised me that no guys were talking to her because she was one of the best-looking girls I'd ever seen. That was before I met Lisa, of course, who even looks better. This girl was wearing a tiny little black French-cut bikini and really knew how to fill out her suit. It was one of the tiniest bikinis I've ever seen, and she sure had a gorgeous body with beautiful dark-brown hair, almost black.

Anyway, I kept wondering about that girl and decided, the hell with it, I'd go over and start talking to her. I wasn't sure how old she was because she looked pretty young and might even have been my age. Approaching her, I wondered what opening line I'd use and as I sat down beside her, just said, "That looks like an interesting book you're reading. What is it?" She lifted her eyes from the book, looked right at me and said, "It's The Bonfire of the Vanities by Tom Wolf. I'm really enjoying it."

"That sounds interesting," I said, trying to get off the subject because I've never even heard of the book or the author, and, in fact, read very little because I don't like to. I didn't want this chick to think I was some kind of moron or something.

I'd heard on a TV talk show that women really appreciate the direct approach, like when a guy comes up and just says, "Hi," then introduces himself and asks the girl her name. In fact, they showed some guys trying to get to know girls using all kinds of different approaches. What the show was trying to prove was that girls don't enjoy hearing a bunch of phony bull crap. What they like instead is when a guy acts like he wants to hear what the girl has to say instead of trying to impress her by being pretentious and bragging and all that. They kept saying nice-looking girls do like nice-looking guys, however. And that morning at the beach I was just wearing my swim trunks and nothing else. I'd left all my punk stuff at home, even the earrings. And before leaving, I worked out with weights so I'd look a bit pumped up on the beach.

Anyway, this girl put aside her book and straightened up a bit to talk, which encouraged me. I told her my name, and she said hers was "Nikki." God, she was cute! Even her name was cute. I was glad she didn't want to talk about literature. So I asked her where she lived and if she came here often. I made some comments about Horny Corner, like the ones I told you about already, and that seemed to get her going pretty well. I guess the advice from the talk show was pretty good because everything worked like a charm.

She told me she used to hang out at Horny Corner. She even met her husband down there. They spent a summer together at the beach and then got married and traveled together for a year in Europe and parts of Asia like Japan, Hongkong and Singapore and places like that. But they found out on their trip that they just couldn't live together. They liked each other, but really didn't love each other. So they dated other people and came back to Horny Corner. They didn't even bother getting divorced or anything because it was too much trouble. If either of them ever wanted to get married again, she said, they'd think about divorcing. In fact, they're still friends but not lovers anymore, though they still go out together now and then. If I was interested, she said, I could see her husband right over there.

She pointed, and I looked over to where this really handsome guy was talking to a couple of girls at the center of Horny Corner. He looked like Brad Pitt, but twenty years younger. That's when I realized this girl was too much for me and started feeling uncomfortable. I wasn't really listening to her anymore, trying to think of some way to exit gracefully. This chick must have been really old, although she sure didn't look it.

The thought came into my head that I could go to the hotdog stand and get us something to eat because it was almost noon. After we had lunch, I'd thank her for the conversation and take off. But then I remembered I only had a couple of bucks, which probably wouldn't be enough to pay for both of us. I didn't know what to do. The conversation was lagging because I wasn't feeding her with questions about herself. She didn't seem to want to know anything about me. And then, just when I was feeling the most uncomfortable, something happened that promised to get me out of this jam. A little guy in a pair of white shorts and a short-sleeved white shirt walked by wearing a little white paper hat like the ones you see at fast-food places. He also had on tennis shoes with no socks, and he was carrying a box in front of him with a strap attached to it hanging from his neck. There were some letters painted on the box, but I couldn't make them out. Well anyway, this guy was yelling at the top of his voice, "Rhubarbs! Try some rhubarbs!" Actually, he was kind of singing it. Without even thinking, I told Nikki that rhubarbs would certainly be a cool thing to have at the beach and if she wanted some, I'd run right over there and get one for her. What I didn't mention, of course, was that it probably wouldn't cost me more than a couple of bucks.

"Excuse me," she said, "but I think he's saying, 'fruit bars' <u>not</u> 'rhubarbs.'" She wasn't laughing or anything and sounded a bit irritated. I didn't say another word, even though I had enjoyed talking to her and hoped to see her down there again sometime. I just picked up my towel and got out of there as fast as I could.

By this time, Paul and I had reached the beach, so we turned right and headed down towards the pier. He was finally talking about something that interested me. The bottom line: he was just as taken with Lora as I was with Lisa and equally puzzled about how to meet her. I had never realized Paul could be so creative or insane, or whatever you want to call it. Because Lora was off limits to him, he'd come up with a plan to get close to her; as weird as it sounds, he'd dressed like a girl.

"But Paul," I objected, "that's crazy! Aren't you afraid people will think you're a queer?"

"I don't care," he said without hesitation. "It'll be worth it if it gets me up close to the girl I love. And besides, no one will ever know it's me."

To be honest, I'd never heard my brother talk this way before. He sounded like a nut rather than the calm and reasonable person I had always known.

"But how will you keep them from finding out?" I asked, more as a challenge than an actual question.

"Easy," Paul said, again without hesitation. "I'll always be wearing a mask. You know, for COVID and stuff."

He had obviously thought this thing through.

"But how will you get her to like you if she doesn't even know it's you?"

And here's where I finally understood the core of his plan. "I will be Paula to find out what Lora needs," my brother explained, "and make sure she gets it. Then, at the right time, I will reenter her life as Paul."

Just when the right time would be, Paul admitted, he didn't yet know.

Turns out, though, that he'd already started putting his plan into motion. Paul (or "Paula," I'm not sure what to call him now) had asked around and found out that Lora was struggling through Sophomore English where they do Shakespeare and world literature and all. It just so happened that Paul had passed his AP English test as a sophomore at our old high school. He knew everything about world literature and all the dead poets and crap, so at the new school they were letting him skip either American Literature or English Literature. They didn't care which, because he'd shown what a wizard he was on the AP English test.

Anyway, because he didn't have to take English, Paul arranged to be a teaching assistant for his science teacher after lunch, which was the same period Lora had Sophomore English. I understand that old Mr. Smith, Paul's science teacher, was pretty cool about everything and didn't even care if Paul hung around or not during the period as long as he could get the correcting done. So now my brother doesn't even go to class at all during his TA period but picks up the work after school just before football practice.

I wouldn't have believed he could be so inventive; I guess this had motivated him like ever before. But all that was just the simple part. The most difficult problem Paul had faced was getting into Lora's English class. To do that, he gambled on the direct approach. He'd heard some things about Miss Perret, Lora's English teacher, that helped. Apparently, she's a drunk who sobers up enough to come to class most of the time, but not always. She's an old lady who's never been married, and if there was ever any romance in her life, well, it's been in the literature she reads. She's an amiable lady, even when she's drunk, and loves her students, Paul told me, but over the years she has tired of teaching and wishes she could find another job.

Paul said he really likes Miss Perret and talks to her as much as he can before and after class to butter her up and all. But she's also a living example of why he'd never want to be a teacher. It's no job for anyone over 40, he says, but when you're over 40 and a teacher, what else can you possibly do? According to Paul, Miss Perret is about 53 and wants to take early retirement in a couple of years. So for now she doesn't listen much to the school administration and just tries to have fun with her students. Sometimes she's so relaxed, Paul said, that she even comes in with a hangover, probably because she wants to save her sick days for some kind of payment when she leaves the place at 55.

Paul tells me Miss Perret is an excellent teacher, even though she can be sarcastic and abrasive with students who give her a hard time. One day after school, he went to see her. I remember a couple of weeks ago, Paul was late to practice, but I was too busy to ask him about it. Anyway, he told her right up front he was in love with a girl in her class. He told her all about how Lora's father wouldn't let her see any guys. He also told her how he planned to dress up like a girl and wondered whether she'd let him audit her class. He told her what an outstanding student he was in English and promised to help Lora get her work done because he'd heard she wasn't doing so well. "I won't actually *do* her work for her," he promised Miss Perret, "just help her understand it. And don't worry about me distracting your class. Everything will just be our little secret."

He assured her he didn't even have to sit next to Lora but would approach her at convenient times during breaks. "There's just one thing I need," Paul said, "and that's a few extra minutes before and after class to change outfits. Can you just let me come in a minute or two late and leave a minute or two early? I'll wear a brace on my leg and act like I'm crippled."

To hear Paul tell it, he just charmed the pants off the old lady. She was eating out of his hand and telling him he could do just about anything he wanted. Paul can be very charming to adults. I've seen nothing like it. As his brother, I can see right through his crap, but anybody over 20 eats it up like cake. I know all this seems improbable, but if you knew Paul like I do, you'd see how he could pull it off.

"The truth is," Miss Perret told Paul, "I'm too old to be doing this job anyway and not sure what I'm accomplishing. If this will help even one student before I retire, well, I guess it's not such a bad thing."

Then she candidly (I think "candidly" was the word Paul used) told him she wasn't afraid of the administration or even parents anymore; they all could just stuff it as far as she was concerned. She had always been interested in drama and playacting, she told him, and really wanted to see whether Paul could pull this off. In fact, she admitted Paul's plan fascinated her. "Let's just think of it as an experiment," she said. "I believe I read about something like this in some old book as an undergraduate. I just don't see how it could do any harm."

Paul seemed like a proper gentleman, the teacher concluded, and even if he got invited to Lora's house, Hudson and the household servants would watch him like a hawk, anyway. I'm sure you think all this sounds weird as hell, but the burned-out old teacher was as interested in doing things her own way as Paul was in doing them *his.* I think both of them wanted to find a way for the strange scheme to work, and the more insane and complicated the experiment, the better they liked it.

And so they made their plan—after checking around to confirm Paul wasn't lying about AP English and being Mr. Smith's TA, Miss Perret gave him the green light. Paul told me there was just one more obstacle he faced, and that was how and where to get in and out of his disguise? Should he do his changing in the boy's restroom or the girl's? Though he'd heard of some schools offering the same restroom for both genders, this one, unfortunately, was not one of them. It wasn't long, though, before he came up with a plan for that too.

Don't forget that one of the fundamental differences between Paul and me is that he has a great rapport with adults, while most of them think I'm nothing but a thug. Even my football coaches, except for Coach Miller, don't talk to me unless it has something to do with the game. It's obvious they think I'm some kind of deviant. My teachers ignore me, but that's probably because I get such poor grades besides dressing the way I do. That Lisa sees through all that crap and considers me a special human being makes me love her even more.

But I was talking about me and my brother. He can con just about any adult, and they think he's the greatest thing since pampers. He went up to old Joe, the grounds supervisor or campus cop or proctor or whatever you want to call him. I always feel uncomfortable talking with adults because I think they know something that I don't, but that's not the case with Paul. He's as comfortable shooting the shit with them as a duck is in the water. No kidding. Anyway, Paul softened up old Joe and started talking to him at lunch.

"Hey Joe," he said, "what's up?"

Joe's a sports fan, there's no doubt about that. He comes to all the varsity football games, and I've seen him at all the pre-season scrimmages, even when he doesn't have to show up. I can tell he's really flattered when any of the varsity football players pay attention to him at all. Maybe Joe was some kind of nerd in high school and now, as an adult, finally talks to the popular kids on campus, I don't know. Anyway, Paul started talking to him, and they discussed lots of things I guess—mainly sports—and suddenly, my brother's so-called "digestive problem" came up. This is a perfect lie, though I'm surprised Paul would try to pull off something so stupid. But he did.

"I have an embarrassing problem that's difficult to talk about," Paul began.

"Hey, no shit," Joe said. "Tell me about it."

"Actually," Paul said, laughing, "it's just the opposite; lots of shit. In fact, it's a never-ending case of Montezuma's Revenge."

Well, you can imagine how that stopped the conversation in its tracks. But just for a minute. "The thing is," Paul went on, "I need a little more time in the restroom, especially right after lunch. Otherwise, well, things get embarrassing."

The food he had to eat at home, Paul explained, just aggravated the problem. Stuff like beans and chili with onions. "You should just thank God you're not Mexican," Paul added with a wink.

Well, he found a sympathetic audience in Joe. And so they arrived at a solution: the campus cop wouldn't kick Paul out of the can after lunch if he needed a little more time. And sure enough, Paul told me, Joe kept his word. Ever since then, just before the late bell rings after lunch, Paul goes to the boy's bathroom and locks himself in a stall to change clothes. When Joe comes by on his rounds and kicks everybody out, Paul sits down and pretends he's using the head. Joe always says, "Is that you, Santos?" and Paul says, "Yes it is," and Joe says, "Are you all right?" and Paul answers, "Yes, I'm fine. I'll be on my way in a minute or two." Then Joe says, "All right. Take care," or something like that, and goes on his merry way. By the time Paul's dressed up, the hall is clear, and no one sees a frumpy-looking girl coming out of the boy's bathroom. Paul says he clumps down the hall as loudly as he can, trying to make a big show that he's late because he's crippled.

It was really great seeing my brother all excited and happy about something. Despite some of what he was saying, I don't think I ever felt closer to him than I did that evening walking down by the bay. I don't mean to say Paul's usually feeling depressed or anything, though he has his moods like everybody else. What I mean is that he's usually very to-the-point and businesslike about everything. He's a "no frills" kind of guy, and I usually think of him as extremely dull, probably because he studies all the time and rarely hangs out with girls. To be honest, I'm probably jealous of his accomplishments.

Now that I'd had time to think about what was going on, though, I felt really bothered by one thing. I had paid little attention to Paula earlier, as I told you, but now I realized I'd never seen a girl dressed in such an out-of-it way as this so-called "Paula" in the Hudsons' backyard.

"Hey, Paul," I said. "I don't enjoy interrupting you when you're going on like this, but how did you go about getting your dress and wig and all?"

He told me he'd gone to the costume shop and to a few thrift stores around town. The whole idea of dressing like a girl was something he'd never thought of before, so all of it had proven challenging.

"You know, Paul," I told him, "you really looked kind of ratty over there at Lora's house. Your hair looked terrible, and you were wearing this out-of-style dress. I really hated looking at you because you looked so bad."

"Right, Mike," he responded, "that's exactly what I wanted. I thought about it a lot and was as inconspicuous as possible. And besides, I had to wear a long skirt because I didn't want to shave my legs."

I told him it surprised me that the Hudson girls would even let him come near their house looking like he did. After all, everyone knew both of them as being among the best-dressed chicks on campus. If he was going to get into it, he might as well do it up right. Why hadn't he let Marty and me help so he could put forth a better appearance and make an impression? What the hell? Why couldn't we all have some fun by doing this together?

If Paul is one thing, it's stubborn. Once he's decided something, it practically takes an act of Congress to get him to consider other options.. He kept insisting he was doing fine and was glad no one noticed him. "I think looking so shoddy helped me get into Miss Perret's class.," Paul said. No heads turned when he came in late and left early. He figured it was because everyone thought he was a poor girl so heavyset and crippled that she didn't merit their interest or notice. As Paula, he could even act intelligent in class without being seen as a

51

threat. "Teachers take lots of flak," Paul said. "I'm doing Miss Perret a favor by helping in her class"

I knew what Paul was talking about because I've often felt that way myself. There seems to be a silent conspiracy in the classroom to go against everything the teacher wants in order to drive him or her crazy. The sooner the better. But I do nothing to help them because teachers haven't exactly done me any favors either and I don't feel like I owe them a thing. I feel sorry for them, but I sure don't feel like helping them either. I figure they make their own beds, so they might as well lie down in them. After all, nobody forced them to be teachers.

I could just see Paul in there sucking up to Miss Perret. He's really the best kiss-ass I've ever seen. But I'll admit that Paul is usually silent in class. I've been in a couple of classes with him and heard what other people say. If he feels sorry for teachers like he says he does, he sure doesn't show it. In that respect, Paul—at least when he's being himself—is like everybody else.

You probably want to know who Marty is. Well—and I've thought about this a lot—she's sort of a girlfriend of mine. I don't mean a lover or anything like that, just a girlfriend, in the literal sense—a *friend* who's a *girl*. She's from my old neighborhood, and we used to hang around together. I haven't seen her since we moved. I've been thinking about calling her, but just haven't gotten around to it. She's one of those girls who's got a beautiful face. I mean it's *really* beautiful, but she's way overweight. I mean *seriously* overweight. Sometimes I think she looks as big as a mountain and should be a woman wrestler or something. If she'd just go on a crash diet, I think she'd be a knockout. Her body isn't too flabby or anything; she seems firm enough, but she's just too big and I really feel uncomfortable when we go downtown together or people see us in public. I'm afraid they'll think I'm some kind of weirdo who's got a fat fetish or something. But Marty isn't obese. At least she isn't too flabby. I know that because sometimes I try to touch her although I don't want her to think I'm doing it on purpose or anything.. When she's done something nice or said something clever, I pat her on the back or slap her on the leg. One time when we were cutting up, I gave her a firm pat on the bottom like you see the guys in sports do on TV. I'm always surprised at how solid she is. I'm not saying she has a good figure, though she's extra-large up top, To be completely honest, I'm really not sure about that because she wears thick sweaters to hide her body and I've never seen her in a bathing suit. All I know is that old Marty is as solid as a rock, and I'd hate to get into a fight with her because I don't know how it would turn out.

I don't really enjoy telling you this, but I sort of love Marty in a weird way. I hope you won't think I'm crazy or anything. I don't think I've ever felt so comfortable around a girl in my life as I do with Marty. Maybe it's because there's nothing sexual going on between us. She's really a kind and intelligent person and fun to be around. We've done many things together that I've never done with anyone else. Like she used to go shopping with me when it was my turn to buy the groceries or when I'd go looking for clothes for myself. And one time we went to an Angels game together. I can't imagine doing things like that with someone I was trying to impress. Being around Marty is just fun. I hate sounding like some male chauvinist or something, but she waits on me hand and foot. If I'm drinking a Coke and seem to be finished with it, she'll ask me if I want another one and, if I do, go get it for me. I really like that kind of attention.

I'm not saying I do nothing for her. Once Dad let me have the car for the evening, and I really didn't feel like putting up with a stressful situation with some chick, so I called up old Marty to see if she'd like going to dinner.

"Sure," she said, "let's go."

"OK, but the restaurant we're going to is a surprise and you've got to dress up"

I thought I'd make a big deal out of it, so I rushed down to the local flower shop before it closed and picked out a nice corsage. Then I called the restaurant down by the harbor and made reservations for "Mr. and Mrs. Santos," and told them it was my wife's birthday. I thought she'd appreciate the joke. When I picked her up, I got out of the car really fast and opened its door for her. She was already standing tall on the sidewalk waiting for me. I say "tall" because she's six-foot-two, about four inches taller than me. She had taken the time to dress up really nicely and fix her hair. And she really has a pretty face, as I've said. "Good evening, m' Lady," I said, bowing and handing her a white orchid. She cracked a big smile and kissed me on the cheek. I don't think she'd ever kissed me before.

"Why thank you, my good sir," she said, doing her best curtsy, which, frankly, was a little shaky. For a moment, I thought she'd fall over.

When we got to the restaurant, she seemed impressed because it was a nice place and expensive too. When I told the guy at the desk that we were Mr. and Mrs. Santos, Marty laughed, but not to make the guy think we were lying or anything. I really like Marty because she has a great sense of humor and can take a joke the way it's intended. The guy at the desk seated us by the window and wished Marty a happy birthday. She seemed to enjoy all this, and we had a terrific view of the boats and ships coming and going along the channel. I don't remember what we ate because all this happened quite a while ago. I think I had duck and Marty probably had prime rib or something. Anyway, after we finished, all the servers came up with this huge chunk of ice cream made up like a monstrous piece of chocolate cake with whipped cream and nuts all over it. There was a lighted candle on it, and the servers sang some goofy song all together about putting another candle on the birthday cake and getting gray hair. After they left, I noticed Marty was tearing up a little and asked what the matter was. "Can't help it," she said, dabbing her eyes. "I'm just happy."

I'd seen women do this on TV now and then, but never in real life. To be honest, I wasn't sure how I felt at that moment, glad or sad?

I've often wondered what it would be like to sacrifice myself and marry Marty, if you can imagine that. Would I be happy? I'd probably end up as one of those jerks who gets sick of his fat wife, ignores her, and starts having affairs with prostitutes or other women who really turn them on. In my case, though, I'd be marrying someone who was fat right from the beginning. So there'd be no excuse for messing around because I should've known what I was getting into.

Now I know you'll think I'm really sick, but I'm tired of lying about everything, so I'll tell you the truth. I have actually imagined being some kind of Dr. Frankenstein or something who could cut off Marty's head and sew it on one of those girls who has a super body but a dog's face. I know you understand what I mean because you've probably seen girls like that all over the place. You wonder how they can have such great bodies and come up so short in the face department. If I could find some chick like that and cut off her head to replace it with Marty's, I'd really be doing both of them a favor. Unfortunately, this fantasy, which I know sounds really gross, wouldn't work anyway because how could this ideal woman live through it? I really wouldn't want to hurt anybody, especially Marty. And even if it could be done, how could I be sure the new girl would have Marty's personality? I wonder if someone's personality is in their head or their body? Maybe I'd have this beautiful-looking woman who ended up having the personality of the dog-faced woman. Maybe she'd be some kind of bitch because people might have been calling her dogface for a long time, and maybe lots of guys took her out just to have sex and then dumped her. I know all this sounds ridiculous, of course, and hope you don't think I'm a pervert. Maybe you've had ideas like this yourself, I don't know.

I've also thought about being married to some super foxy chick with an impressive face and body but all stuck on herself; someone I really didn't like too much. I'd make love to her a lot because she looked so nice, but I wouldn't want to talk to her because she was so conceited. So I'd go over to Marty's place to talk and cut up and go shopping or watch movies and baseball games. Kind of as if Marty were a second wife. I hear they do things like that in Utah or Saudi Arabia, and they used to do it a lot in the Bible. It makes sense because there are more women in the world than men, I hear, and three people can live together more cheaply than one or two as long as they all get along. I really think I could make love to Marty if we were on a deserted island and there were no other women around. But then what if we got rescued and had to go home? I wonder what effect that would have on Marty? This is all too much, and I'm really getting off track.

So anyway, Paul was telling me how he finally contacted Lora in their English class. "I just went over and sat down next to her," he said. Of course, he'd waited for the perfect opportunity, which came one day when Miss Perret got tired of her students' complaints about having to read boring old *Romeo and Juliet*. Why didn't Shakespeare, they wanted to know, write so they could understand? Miss Perret got so frustrated that she stopped and gave the class 20 minutes of free time. And that's when Paul made his move. "No one else was talking to her," he said, "and I actually thought she looked lonesome. So I went over and said hello. I didn't even feel embarrassed about being dressed as a girl; I just spoke quietly and very low."

Most of the other kids think this "Paula" character is a kind of nut job anyway, Paul said, but a happy one who they accept and even _like_ while paying her very little attention. I wonder if you've ever had a kid like that in class. He or she is a kind of weirdo or goofball. They do strange things like wear Santa Claus hats at Christmastime or put bells on their shoes or something. You know they'll do things that the cool kids on campus would rather die than do. And they're really intelligent too, maybe even geniuses. They're kind of teacher's pets and talk a lot in class. Sometimes they even put down the other students, but they have a knack for getting away with it.

I remember a guy named Bradford who'd always sit up front in a boring English class I took. The teacher claimed to have a PhD, and often the rest of us thought he was just teaching Bradford. Sometimes, class would start 15 minutes late because the teacher was talking to Bradford. Then the two of them would get together at lunch and talk even more. Anyway, I remember one time around Christmas when Bradford came to class wearing a Santa Claus hat, like I was saying before, and he had a bumper sticker on his notebook that said, "It sure is hard to soar like an eagle when you flock around with a bunch of turkeys." This one guy, a big tackle on the football team, didn't like that, I guess, and got really mad.

"Hey, Bradford," he demanded, "are you saying that we're a bunch of turkeys?"

Bradford turned his head, looked right at him, and said, "Yeah, that's right. You're all a bunch of turkeys, but I still love you." The guy just said, "OK, Bradford," and went back to his seat. Bradford's response was pretty sarcastic, but he got away with it anyway. Some other kids, if they acted like that, would get the piss beat out of them. I know this is true because I've seen it happen.

Anyway, I guess Paul came off like that and was even pretty popular in a weird sort of way. So when he sat down next to Lora, it didn't put her off and even seemed to cheer her up. "How do you like this class?" he asked her.

"Well," she said, "it's all right and the people are nice. But I really hate Shakespeare and don't understand _Romeo and Juliet_ at all. I'm worried about the upcoming test. If everything in here is as dense as this, I might fail the class."

That gave Paul the perfect opening.

"Tell you what," he said in his best Paula voice, "I'm pretty good at this stuff and can help."

That immediately brightened Lora's mood. She invited him to her house the very next Saturday, which was the same day Paul and I were having this conversation. They were supposed to spend a few hours working on *Romeo and Juliet* together but then Stephanie came over, and since Stephanie was also one of Lisa's friends, they all took a break and were talking about the game when I showed up, as I told you before.

Now Paul wanted to know how I got into the backyard and why I'd looked like a gardener. So I told him everything without holding back because, for the first time in his life, my little brother seemed to open up to me.

Paul was very pleased with himself about the way things were going. Apparently, he and Lora had talked all about Paul Santos in their free time, and they've said a lot more about him than I heard that morning. I guess Lora is a lot more hung up on Paul than she had let on. Evidently Paul, disguised as Paula, has become her confidant. And apparently Lora doesn't feel like she has to put on airs around Paula the way she does around her other girlfriends. Sort of like how I feel around Marty. I guess Lora's told "Paula" that she thinks Paul Santos is so good-looking that when she sees him, she just wants to break out and cry. Yes, really, *cry*. She knows Paul has a rep for being a snob and keeping to himself, but she's sure anyone who looks as kind as he does must be really nice. She just wishes there was some way to get to know him that wouldn't be too awkward or embarrassing.

Paul tells me the situation has tempted him many times to pull off his wig and reveal who he really is. But the right moment has not yet arrived. If he did it in class, he's not sure what the reaction would be. Since he's kind of popular—practically worshipped, in fact, by some of the younger sophomores—he's sure word would quickly spread. He's afraid he'd get poor Miss Perret in trouble, or maybe worse, like Lora would resent being fooled. We both agreed that we didn't exactly know what we were getting into or how we'd get out of trouble if things really went bad. We both had this silly idea that it was going too good for us, like Fate was lending its hand. But then we dropped that part of the conversation because we were sounding like a couple of drips, and I think both of us were getting scared.

I told Paul I planned to call Marty when I got home. Of course he knew her, though when she used to come around the apartment in our old neighborhood, he'd ignore her and act like she wasn't even there. One time I got really pissed at him and said, "Aren't you going to say hi to Marty?" And he said, "Hi, Marty," then went into his room without even trying to be cordial. Later I chewed him out for being so stuck up. No wonder he has a reputation for being a snob. I knew about his ambition to be class president and told him if he expected to run for office, he'd better pay attention to people like Marty because she had a vote, just like everybody else. He just said "OK" and went back into his room. I remember standing there even madder than before. Paul sure enjoyed dishing out lectures but couldn't stand hearing one himself.

Anyway, I told him as much about Marty as he needed to know. What I didn't tell him was all that kinky stuff I told you because, well, I've said nothing like that to anyone in my life before now. So I'd appreciate if you'd just pretend you're deaf and didn't hear it. "Marty's pretty big," I told him. "She probably has all kinds of clothes around to fit you. Maybe even a few expensive wigs. And she really knows how to do up her face to make it very appealing. She can probably do the same thing for you."

He already was aware, of course, that I too know a few things about fixing hair. I could see now that he was really listening. It's interesting that Paul has never made fun of my being into this cosmetology stuff like some other guys have. It's almost as if he respects what I do—kind of like he understands this could be the one avenue open to me to make a living. It's like he doesn't want to say anything discouraging because I know for a fact both he and Dad think if I don't get myself straightened out pretty soon I won't have any choice but to end up on welfare, in jail, or in the army or something.

"Well, don't make me *too* attractive," Paul said with a wink in his voice. "I don't want to attract too much attention."

"OK," I said, "but I'll bet you'll get to spend more time with Lora if you look nicer in drag. I don't think you realize how important clothes are to these people. They put a lot of emphasis on looking good." I knew that from the experience of working with quite a few of their girlfriends at the beauty shop.

By now, we had reached the pier. I can't believe what a seed-bag hangout this place has become in the last couple of years. There was a bathhouse for homos just around the corner they had closed down after people started complaining. The area still looked like one big dump with paper and trash all over. You hardly ever saw anyone decent looking around there—just homeless people and drug addicts. It seemed like every refugee in the world sat fishing along the pier. I hope you don't think I'm into making racist comments or anything. I mean, I guess my father was a refugee, and America is a sort of country of refugees, if you think about it. The people on the pier are just poor. I don't consider them dirty or immoral or anything. They just fish and pick aluminum cans out of the trash because they have to.

Anyway, the pier is really filthy. There's trash everywhere, as I told you before, and there are squashed fish everywhere and the place smells like hell. It doesn't seem like the city gives a damn about any of that. Maybe it's because most of the people there are poor and don't matter because they don't pay taxes or anything. I remember something about "the cycle of poverty" I heard about in one of my classes. Don't ask me to explain it, because I'm not sure exactly what it means. It just seems like an appropriate thing to think about when you're in a place like this.

There were lots of tough-looking people hanging out all over the place, and I started feeling a little uncomfortable. I knew I didn't look too out-of-it there because there were lots of people around who dress like me. But Paul stuck out like a sore thumb, looking all "pretty-boy" and preppy and stuff. Suddenly it occurred to me that some of Sandy's brothers might be around, and I got all nervous and broke into a sweat.

"Hey, it's getting pretty late," I told Paul. "This isn't exactly a good place to be after dark."

"Hey, no biggie," he replied. "Let's just walk out to the end of the pier."

When we got there, we both sort of slouched over the railing and looked out at the ocean. I don't know whether either of us really saw it, though, because we were both so lost in our own thoughts. We looked out over the water because that's what you do when you get to the end of a pier, I guess.

"I've really enjoyed our talk," Paul said. "It's great to have a brother like you who gets how I feel."

Then he pushed himself back away from the railing and looked right at me like you see some guys do with their girls in the movies. He grabbed me by the shoulders and gave me a hug. It scared me to death because I thought he would kiss me. I didn't know what to do—he'd done nothing like this in all the years I'd known him. I felt so embarrassed, in fact, that I actually began praying that none of the thugs around would notice what we were doing. I don't know how long he kept holding me, but it seemed like hours or a lifetime or something like that. Finally, he let go and I don't think I ever felt so relieved in my life. But I was still afraid someone had seen us. I looked around and noticed that no one seemed to act funny, laughing, or doing anything unusual. They all seemed intent on their fishing, or whatever they were doing, and some kids were running all over the place throwing seaweed at each other.

Paul said, "What do you think about all this, buddy?"

I said, "What do you mean—about *what*?" I really didn't know what he was talking about. He'd never called me "buddy" before.

"I mean all this about Lora and Lisa and what we've been doing and all."

"Oh, that," I said, somewhat relieved. "I really don't know what to think about it." I didn't know what he was getting at.

"Well, Mike, let's go ahead with the thing you want to do with Marty. Like you said, if we're going to do something as crazy as this, we might as well do it up right."

I wasn't sure how I felt now that he was talking about what *we* were going to do instead of what *he* was going to do.

"Can we agree on one thing, buddy?" he went on. "Can we agree to help each other out in this, so if one of us gets in a jam, the other can try to pull him out and make things go smoothly?"

"Sure," I said. I was glad to hear this. "I'll do all I can to help you, if you do all you can to help *me.*" I offered my hand for him to shake on it.

After that, I suggested we head home. I was eager to get off this pier as soon as possible. As we walked back down towards the other end, I saw some people giving us tough looks, especially Paul. But he didn't seem to notice. I looked all around to see if any of Sandy's brothers or friends were there, but didn't see any. When we got to the base of the pier, I asked Paul if he wanted to race me home. He was always eager to enter competitions like this and took off without saying another word. But I passed him without too much trouble and stayed ahead of him the rest of the way. I could hear him huffing and puffing behind me, and even slowed down twice so he wouldn't get discouraged and quit. Paul was an excellent runner, but I always had the edge on him in that department.

Chapter Five

The next Saturday I went over to the Hudson's house bright and early, dressed up in my gardener's outfit. I was eager to get into their yard, thinking that Lisa might be there. I had bought a toy for Maria's kids called "Alligator Alley." It was one of those slip n' slide type toys, only this one wasn't all dangerous like the ones you read about on the internet. I checked it out carefully. On the box it says something about being a new-and-improved design approved as safe by some magazine or parents' group or something.

"Hey," I asked the salesman, "mind if I open it up and take a look?"

"No problemo, amigo," the guy said. He must have noticed I was Mexican and thought he was being cute.

Anyway, the only place you fasten the thing to the ground is at the beginning, where the kids start their run. And they made the fasteners out of plastic, not metal. The part where the kids end up after sliding doesn't fasten to the ground at all. Instead, you attach a hose to an opening in the toy, creating a little swimming pool where the kids end up after sliding down the plastic ramp. There was also this plastic thing that looked like a hula hoop, if your dad or grandma ever told you what one of those things was. On this new toy, you're supposed to cut out a plastic drape with the picture of an alligator on it and sling it over the hula hoop thing somehow to straddle the plastic gangway. The kids are supposed to slip on down under the hula hoop and through the alligator drape and into the little swimming pool at the end. It looked like lots of fun.

The toy set me back quite a few bucks, but I thought it was worth it because anything I could do to butter up Maria might help later. I was learning a few tricks from Paul. I didn't mind spending money on Maria's kids, anyway. In fact, even if I spent everything I earned at the Hudsons' on those kids, I wouldn't mind. I really like them, especially the little girl. It's almost like she's my kid now that I saved her life and all. Wait, why don't you forget I just said that, ok? I know it sounds weird, so please just forget it.

Anyway, when I got there, nobody was in the backyard. I didn't have to go through the garage door because Alihandro had shown me where they hid the key that opened a gate in the wall. I hadn't really noticed it until he showed me. I looked all around to make sure no one was watching before picking up the rock where they'd hidden the key. When I got into the backyard, I set up the toy I'd bought for the kids. It really wasn't difficult. I got all the tools I needed from the shed Alihandro had shown me the week before. I hadn't paid much attention the first time I saw it, but now noticed that the building hadn't always been a tool shed. It was actually quite spacious and charming and neat. Alihandro kept the place tidy, and there was even a little daybed out there where he would go take a few winks when Maria was cranky and he wanted to get out of the house. Otherwise, the entire family—Al, Maria and the two kids—stayed in the main house in a section reserved just for them. This tool shed would really make a nice bachelor's apartment if someone just added a stove and shower and all.

When I finished setting up the Alligator Alley, I knocked on the back door, and Maria seemed glad to see me. "Look what I got for the kids!" I said. They were already playing behind Maria, tangled in her skirts and trying to see what was going on.

"Wow, really?" she said, looking past me into the yard. "That's so sweet!"

I guess she didn't mind because the kids were in their swimsuits in an instant and sliding down the ramp like pros in no time at all.

"Hey Maria," I blurted, "can you get me a couple of buckets of hot water?"

I asked because I remembered when my brother and I were kids we had this stupid little plastic swimming pool, and my father would put a few buckets of hot water in it to warm things up. You wouldn't believe how good it felt. And, sure enough, the kids screamed with delight after I warmed up the swimming pool section of the Alligator Alley. I put my hand in the water to make sure it wasn't too hot and it felt just like bathwater.

"Please," they begged almost in unison, "come and slide with us!"

I pretended not to hear, hoping they'd drop it and just continue having a good time without me. But they kept it up. It's funny they could speak English a lot better than their parents, even though they were just little kids. They kept nagging me and just wouldn't give up. The truth is, though, that they were talking to the right person because I'm really just a kid at heart and would do anything for a laugh, no matter how silly. So, without thinking about it anymore, I took off down the little ramp with my ski cap, army jacket, boots, and everything else on, and ended up getting soaked like crazy in the little swimming pool. Alihandro was there now too, and he and Maria and the kid laughed their heads off. Then Maria went back into the house, came out an instant later with a bunch of towels and started dabbing me off. She pulled at my ski cap, but I held onto it, not wanting anyone to see my weird hair. I didn't know what it would look like all wet and stuffed up under a knit ski cap. Just to be safe, I refused to take off my army jacket too,

"Don't worry about me," I told Maria. "I've got to get back to work."

I was pleased with myself for making such a big hit with the kids and their parents, but hoped Lisa hadn't seen me. Unfortunately, though, looking up at the door, I saw her standing there laughing her head off with the rest of them.

I spent quite a few hours puttering around in the flower beds trying to level out the ground around where they had built the wall. Then I planted some shrubs Maria had bought during the week. Suddenly, I noticed Paul had arrived and was sitting with Lora over on the patio working on Romeo and Juliet. I guess I should just call him (or her) *Paula* here because that's how everyone saw her. Anyway, they were reading their parts aloud, with Paula taking the part of Romeo and Lora playing Juliet. At that moment, Paula was reading some silly speech from the play that might get young lovers all excited:

Two of the fairest stars in all the heaven,
Having some business, do entreat her eyes
To twinkle in their spheres till they return.
What if her eyes were there, they were in her head?
The brightness of her cheek would shame those stars
As daylight doth a lamp; her eyes in heaven
Would through the airy region stream so bright
That birds would sing and think it were not night.
See how she leans her cheek upon her hand!
Oh, that I were a glove upon that hand,
That I might touch that cheek!

IT DIDN'T SEEM LIKE LORA WAS HAVING ANY TROUBLE understanding the play. In fact, it looked like the two of them were having a great time cutting up and everything else. Old Shakespeare would probably have rolled over in his grave if he could see what they were doing to his play. But they were having a merry time of it and really seemed to be enjoying themselves.

I noticed that Paula really looked a lot better than she had before. When I'd called Marty on Saturday night, she'd been eager to come over on Sunday morning. Up front, I told her what we were doing. I mean, I told her right up-front what *Paul* was doing. I didn't say anything about me and Lisa because Marty might not understand. Wait, that's not exactly right. What I mean is that she might understand completely, which would probably hurt her feelings and all. I'm pretty sure she likes me in the romantic sense a lot more than I like her, and I respect her enough to not hurt her feelings unless I really have to.

Anyway, Marty brought over a lot of stuff, including some wigs and all that. I always thought of her as kind of a poor girl, but she seemed to have enough bucks to buy herself really nice clothes. I think she realized she didn't have the best body in the world, so may as well package herself as best she could. Her family must have had some money somewhere or another. She works at a department store and gets discounts, but she doesn't just shop *there* and I've never seen a girl spend as much money on clothes as she does, not even Lisa and Lora.

We put some of her old things on Paul. My father was out visiting Mom's grave like he did every Sunday morning. Marty called these clothes "old things," even though they were right in style and everything else. They were a little big and baggy on Paul, though he didn't look bad in them at all. Marty taught Paul how to put on a bra because, as Marty said, "Paul, to tell you the truth, you're just a little flat-chested." All of us laughed at that, but I think guys, no matter who they are, have a kind of wary respect for bras. I mean, if you're a guy and you ever take one off a girl, you're really in trouble if you've never done it before. And just about the time you get used to taking them off, they invent a new bra that comes undone at the front or the side or doesn't come undone at all. I don't care what kind of bra she's wearing. Unless you're working with a girl who really wants you to get her bra off, you're never going to succeed at it no matter how hard you try. I don't care how experienced you think you are. I'm sure glad guys don't have to wear anything like that.

Anyway, Marty was pretty successful at teaching Paul how to take the bra on and off. He's really a fast learner, I'm surprised. At first, he had trouble because he's pretty muscular, and the bra Marty brought over only fastened at the back. She left all the other kinds at home. He had some difficulty at first trying to make his hands work behind his back, but pretty soon he got the hang of it, and Marty told him that a girl couldn't have done any better.

All the skirts and dresses Marty brought over were long, but, in every case, showed a little of Paul's leg. Marty and I decided he had to shave them, and man, did he put up a fuss! He was worried about what the guys would say in the locker room when they saw his bare legs. "Just tell 'em you tape up your socks for games and are tired of pulling out hairs with the tape," I suggested. "Believe me, they'll soon forget about it."

Eventually, he consented. Marty and I showed him how to use a lady's razor without cutting himself. Marty had thought ahead enough to bring hers, something I hadn't thought of myself.

Then came the makeup. Admittedly, Marty knew a lot more about leg shaving and bras than I did, but I was her equal, or maybe even her better, regarding makeup. I had to learn all about it in beauty school.

When we were done with that, we pulled out all the wigs Marty brought over. She had about five. We tried to pick out one about the same color as the old, ragged wig Paul had bought at the thrift store. Luckily, there was one not too different, even though it was nice and not a piece of crap like the one Paul bought. We put the wig on Paul's head, and that's when I took over. As I told you before, I have a genuine talent for working on a girl's hair.

Then we looked through the shoes Marty brought. I can't believe it, but she wore just about the same size Paul did. I never thought about that before. It wasn't a problem at all. I guess a girl as big as Marty has to have some pretty enormous feet to hold up all that weight. And then Marty noticed something we had missed. We needed to put pantyhose on Paul. He'd have to take off his skirt to put on the pantyhose, and he did it with no hassle. In fact, we were all laughing and cutting up, and Paul really seemed to get into it. When everything was on him, he looked strikingly attractive—like a real girl and a good-looking one at that.

"Hey girl, you look pretty sexy!" I said, making Paul blush.

I've heard stories about guys picking up hookers who they think are girls, but really are guys. I think they call them transvestites or transgenders, or something like that. Anyway, they look so feminine the guy thinks he's getting a boiling hot partner. He's in for an enormous surprise, though, (sometimes _really_ enormous, if you know what I mean) when the moment of truth finally comes. I read about one guy in the Philippines—a US Marine, I think—who was so surprised that he lost his cool, killed the "girl," and had to spend a lot of time in prison. When I saw what a convincing girl my brother, Paul, made, I really understood how that could happen.

Anyway, we all kept on laughing after dragging Paul in front of a mirror, but I think we also felt a little scared that maybe we had created something we wouldn't be able to control.

As all this was going on, Paul kept talking to me a lot more than usual. It seemed like our walk down to the pier had been some kind of turning point in our relationship. We were much better friends after that walk and the run that followed.

The next day he told me everyone in Miss Perret's class turned to look at him as he walked in the door. "I think they thought I was sexy," Paul said. "God only knows what they'd think if they knew…"

After class, he said he talked to Lora, who even commented on how good he looked. The way he described it, her eyes sparkled as she told him what a good-looking girl he was and that she hadn't noticed it before. Then she asked Paul to come over next Saturday to study, and he accepted the invitation with pleasure.

That's the same day I spent in the flower beds trying to make the place look good. If there was anything I could do to beautify Lisa's place, I certainly would try my best. I felt happy with what I'd accomplished so far, but also hungry. I looked at my watch and saw that it was almost 12:30., but then decided to keep working until it was time to go home. Paul and Lora were eating something on the patio, and I felt contented, as if we were all one big, happy family working on the same thing together. I'd never felt that way before because I'd never had a mother or sister or little kids in my family. When my brother and I were growing up, we never really thought of ourselves as little kids.

Suddenly, I heard someone coming up behind me. It was Lisa holding a tray with some sandwiches, potato chips and Pepsis on it. It looked like enough food for both of us. "Are you hungry?" she asked and, I swear, there was a twinkle in her eye.

"Sure," I said. Frankly, she had caught me off guard and I didn't know what else to say.

She walked over to a love seat in the shade and gestured for me to come join her. By now my clothes had dried so I felt more comfortable than I had a couple of hours earlier. Still, I knew I was a mess to look at and was glad to be wearing a mask.

I don't remember talking very much during lunch. I don't enjoy talking with my mouth full, especially with someone like Lisa. And I was nervous about pulling my mask down, so tried to avoid looking at her directly using the excuse, when necessary, of having a mouth full of food. Whenever she asked me something, I'd point to my mouth and laugh, and she seemed to understand and laugh too. To be honest, I've always had the habit of putting too much food in my mouth. You couldn't be a dainty eater around guys like my brother and dad unless you wanted to starve to death. Anyway, this bad habit now seemed to help me by literally providing a cover.

She asked all kinds of questions, and I really had a hard time answering because the stories just weren't coming as quickly as usual. I won't tell you what all I said to her because they were just a bunch of lies..

"Hey, do you know anything about algebra?" she asked suddenly as soon as we finished lunch. "I'm having a hard time with my homework, and Paula and Lora are too busy to help."

"I took a little last year," I told her, this time speaking the truth, "but I'm really not very good at it."

She said she'd go get her book anyway, and maybe I'd remember how to do the stuff that was giving her trouble. When she brought the book out, I felt panicky like I'd screw up and she'd find out that I was really an imbecile. I just hoped I could concentrate enough to help. She gave me the book, open to the pages containing the challenging problems.

"Show me the steps," I said, trying to hold down my panic. "I'm afraid I'm a little rusty."

Without a word, she took the book back and found the right page. I read over the explanation three times. I don't think anything went into my head the first time because I was too nervous and upset. But on the third reading, something clicked, and I suddenly recognized this as one part of algebra that I really understood. I wasn't very good at it; I'm telling the truth because I got a "C" in the course which, for me, is way above average. But I also remember that some of the other students, even the good ones, had difficulty with this lesson. And yet, for some weird reason, the whole concept was as clear as day to me both then and now since I'd just reread the explanation. This all took some time, but Lisa sat there patiently waiting for me to finish. I felt she was studying my face curiously as I read. I don't know why. When I finished, we turned back to where the problems were, and I showed her how to do them.

"I get it!" she said suddenly, with an excitement so exaggerated that it almost seemed like she was messing with me. "Thank you so much. I think I can take it from here." Then she stood up, grabbed the book, and said, "If you ever have a problem with anything—*anything* at all—I'd be more than glad to help."

I immediately took her up on her offer. I still can't believe I had the courage to do that when I hardly even knew her but, without hesitating, I told her there was something she could help me with right now.

Lisa sat back down and appeared to be all ears.

"This is really embarrassing," I began, "but at school there's this beautiful girl who's all high class and rich but nice and I'm afraid to approach her for a conversation. You're a girl—maybe you could give me some hints.."

It amazed me that these words were coming out of my mouth. I don't know why, but they seemed to flow out of me naturally..

Lisa didn't answer right away but looked very thoughtful. Then she started telling me about what girls like and don't like. My ears pricked up when she started talking about her own personal preferences when guys come onto her, which, I imagine, happens a lot.

"I love receiving little gifts from guys," she said, "like flowers and cards and stuff. It doesn't have to be expensive or anything, one flower is enough. What a girl really likes are little tokens that a guy is thinking of her."

To make a long story short, she confirmed what the TV talk show had said about girls preferring the direct approach. They don't appreciate all kinds of clever opening lines. Sure they like guys to say witty thing and be funny and all, but they don't like it when a guy is *trying* to be clever and acting all unnatural and uptight

Then she said something that really surprised me. "These days," she said, "a girl is just as obligated to be open and honest with a guy she likes as guys should be with girls *they* like. I don't know why girls think they have to act all perverse and disinterested when a guy they like comes around."

I distinctly remember her using the word "perverse." I know I'm not mistaken.

"It's harder for a girl to meet a guy than for a guy to meet a girl," Lisa went on. She didn't mean to suggest that guys have it easy, she said. She knew they act all macho and do stupid stuff to impress girls, then try not to act hurt if they get rejected. Guys feel the same way girls do when they get put down hard, she said. She didn't mean to imply otherwise. It's just that today girls are told so many contradictory things. They're told not to be like girls used to be, all shy and stuff. Nowadays they can go up to guys they like and just start talking, even if they don't know them. In fact, girls today are even told they can ask strange guys out. I mean, let's face it, things have gotten so weird now that girls can even choose to *be* guys, if they want and, of course, that goes both ways.

Yet some people still tell them to act like ladies and not be forward because it'll give the wrong idea like they're sluts or hussies or something. I'm paraphrasing what Lisa said and have added a few thoughts of my own. I'll leave it to you to figure out which thoughts are mine and which are hers. Anyway, she put it all much better than I can, though I'm doing my best to give you the drift. I have a pretty good vocabulary, but nothing like Lisa's.

"I wish I could practice what I preach," she said. "Guy/girl relationships have always been hard and will go on being hard no matter what they tell you. It's like some perverse" (there was that word again) "cat-and-mouse game that eventually brings grief to everybody."

Take her for example. She was all hung up, she told me, on some senior at her school. This guy was an outstanding athlete and very nice-looking, but kept to himself, which a lot of her friends thought was weird. He wasn't much of a student and all that, but he was different and interesting and probably a deep human being. She used the word "deep." That was her exact word. She knew he was creative because some of her girlfriends had been to the beauty salon where he works. But she just couldn't figure out how to get to know him. He was a senior, and she was only a sophomore. He probably didn't even know she existed.

To be honest, I felt so stunned that I didn't hear much after that.

She'd told me a lot about herself and I'd really felt comfortable in her presence and had loved talking to her until near the end, when she started talking about *me*. I knew it was me, and my mouth got kind of dry and my throat pretty hoarse. I realized I might go too far but couldn't stop myself from speaking.

"A girl who believes as you do," I said, "should introduce herself to the guy she likes." In fact, I advised, she shouldn't worry about it anymore at all, but just do what some of her girlfriends did and skip class on Monday to march right over to that beauty salon and get acquainted with the guy. She didn't have to act all forward or anything, I said. All she had to do was go over there, let him work on her hair and just start talking naturally. If things worked out, they worked out. If the guy was a creep or a jerk, well, she'd find that out too.

Just then, Lora came running up. Lisa had a call, she said, and it was Stephanie. I'll never understand how someone can be deeply involved in a conversation and the phone rings and she runs off at the drop of a hat to talk to the person on the phone, leaving the first person just hanging. Well, that's exactly what Lisa did. She thanked me, but said she had to run. I don't think she meant anything bad by it, she's just conditioned to do this like everybody else.

After Lisa left, I went back to work. I felt glad to have something in my stomach but, to tell the truth, by 12:30 was wondering whether I could make it through the day with no more food. Still, I just kept working in the flower beds, thinking about how all this would work out. I couldn't believe that, out of all the guys at school, she'd be interested in me. I know this sounds goofy, but I felt like the luckiest guy in the world.

About 3:30 p.m. I knocked off for the day. Old Hudson didn't seem to care what time I quit or even if I showed up. He didn't even seem interested in what I was doing in his yard. I promised myself, though, that I wouldn't take advantage of him even if it was easy to do. I would keep an accurate accounting of my hours and try not to cheat. Then, just as I was about to leave the yard and start walking home, Lisa popped out of the house smiling brightly and telling me how much she enjoyed our conversation. She was sorry about having to jump up and run to the phone. She really is a thoughtful girl, Lisa is.

Then she said Daddy had given her permission to go to the beach the next day. I guess "daddy" was old Mr. Hudson. Maria would take them, and Lora and Paula would go and perhaps Stephanie would come too. Alihandro wouldn't go because something else demanded his attention. Anyway, she wondered whether I wanted to come along. I could be her bodyguard, she said. She laughed when she said this, though not in any sexually suggestive way or anything. She said Daddy told her it was OK and would even pay for my time.

I said sure I'd like to go, and what time did she want me to show up? I was excited as hell but tried not to show it. She told me to come on over around 9:30 a.m. and we'd all leave about a quarter to ten or ten o'clock. I said, "OK, see you then," and left right away, thinking if I hung around and kept talking, she might change her mind.

On my way home, I thought about being Lisa's bodyguard. "Bodyguard" was exactly the word she used, I'm sure of it. And then I started thinking about Lisa's body and how I'd give almost anything to see her in a bathing suit. And how, in fact, that's exactly what I'd be doing the next day if I could make it home and back to her place without getting hit by a car or something. I stopped at each street corner and looked carefully both ways before crossing. I hoped I could remember to do the same thing tomorrow, going the opposite direction.

Honestly, I don't think I'd ever been happier than I was as I walked home that day. I could feel my heart beating and felt all gushy inside. I even wanted to sing a corny love song that kept running through my mind. I know I'm talking about personal things now, which sounds stupid as hell, so I'd appreciate if you wouldn't tell anyone what I'm saying. I felt ready to explode with love and happiness and really wanted to kiss someone. At that moment, I didn't even care who it was. This half-way good-looking girl was walking my way on the other side of the street, and I had an almost uncontrollable urge to run over there, kiss her right on the mouth, then run away before she could respond. I didn't do it, though I sure felt like it.

I kept on walking and saw a couple of kids playing hopscotch on the sidewalk. They'd drawn the hopscotch thing on the sidewalk and were jumping all over the place, even on the lines. They didn't seem to care. I said, "Hi, kids! How are you today, having lots of fun?" They sort of looked at me strangely as if to say, "Who do you think you are?" You know how everyone teaches school kids these days not to talk to strangers and say "No" to everything. They looked at me like I was some kind of pervert. I looked at the pieces of chalk spread all over the sidewalk, hoping to see one that was yellow. Right then, I had a crazy impulse to draw a smiley face or something right on the sidewalk. But there wasn't any yellow chalk. Maybe they'd think I was a cool guy and smile and talk to me instead of thinking I was a pervert. But then I remembered the clothes I'd put on. I really looked like a migrant farm worker, for Chrissakes! All these good people around here would have to do is see a seedy-looking Mexican guy scrawling graffiti across the sidewalk, and they'd surely call the cops and get me into real trouble. I might even have to spend the night in the tank or something. Then I started worrying about the trouble that could come my way, kissing strangers, talking to little kids and writing on sidewalks, and decided I'd better cool it.

And that's when I started feeling depressed. What if all this didn't end up the way I hoped it would? Like tomorrow, for instance, how was I going to bring off this beach thing? People don't exactly wear blue-knit ski caps to the beach unless it's freezing like in the winter. In fact, it had been unseasonably warm lately, as the newspapers said, and that's why we were going to the beach in September. What was I going to do about my hair? I didn't know, so I figured I'd better get a haircut. I thought I'd better hurry because all the barber shops would close pretty soon, and they wouldn't be open early enough on Sunday.

I ran all the way home, turned left, and headed down to the little street in town that had all the stores on it. When I got to the barbershop I knew was there, I walked right in and told them I wanted a flattop cut sort of close on the sides. I don't think I put much thought into this, and I'd never been to this shop before.

When I got home, I went right to the bathroom. Dad was busy with something or the other. I don't remember what it was. Before I'd left the barbershop, I'd put my cap back on. I wasn't sure how this haircut would look, and didn't want anyone, especially someone I knew, to see me with it. Anyway, in the bathroom, I walked right up to the mirror and took off the cap. My hair didn't look bad at all. I admit I looked like some kind of Marine or something, but Marine haircuts weren't exactly out of style there, since we weren't too far from a military base. In fact, I'm really glad guys today can wear different haircuts. They don't have to wear long hair anymore, unless they want to, and they can even shave their heads and be OK too. Dad has told me lots of times that Mom used to say I had a nice-shaped head. When you don't know your mother very well like I don't know mine, you remember things she said before or, more often, things other people tell you she said. She also said I had pretty feet for a boy, but that doesn't have anything to do with what we're talking about, so you can just forget I said it.

I wasn't sure I looked like a punk anymore. Maybe I looked more like a skinhead or something. I didn't know, and I didn't really care. It's funny, but ever since I'd started liking Lisa, whether I looked like a punk hadn't been as important as before.

Don't get me wrong, I'm not moralizing. I'm definitely not saying there's anything wrong with looking like a punk or that this super-classy chick reformed me or anything. What I'm trying to say is that it didn't really matter to me anymore whether I looked like a punk, even though I liked the look as much as ever.

Then I started worrying about what trunks I'd wear the next day, but I won't bore you with the details.

Chapter Six

I woke up early the next morning because, to tell the truth, I was too excited to sleep. The conversation Lisa and I had the day before kept ringing in my head. I remembered her saying girls are into things like cards and flowers, and it didn't matter how expensive they were or anything. So I took a piece of white paper out of my desk and looked for the set of watercolors I kept there too. With water from the bathroom, I went to work on an abstract design, taking up half the paper. I'm pretty good at art, if I may say so myself. When I finally felt satisfied with the painting, I folded the paper in half with the design on the outside and thought about what to write inside. Many gushy love things came to mind, but they all seemed inappropriate. I wanted to say something simple. That's not as easy as you might think. Lots of the things came to mind, but they were too stupid or as inappropriate as those gushy love things. Finally, I wrote "Dear Lisa, Thanks for the conversation yesterday. It's really nice to have a friend I can talk to. Sincerely, Manuel." It wasn't as good as the design, but it would have to do because I couldn't think of anything else..

Then I went out to the backyard. There was a little rose garden there, and I didn't think the landlord would mind if I copped just one little rose. I found a perfect one. It was a little red rosebud just coming out, and it had no bugs on it or anything like that.

I walked back into the house and noticed it was already 9:15 a.m. I figured I'd better get going, or I'd be late. I didn't want them to leave without me because I wasn't sure what beach they were going to. I hurriedly looked around for an envelope but couldn't find one big enough, so I folded the card in half again to make it smaller, though I knew that would look stupid. Finally, I put the card into the envelope and wrote "Lisa" on the outside.

I already had on my gardener's outfit, so I didn't have to worry about that. My trunks were on underneath. I was just about to leave the apartment when I remembered my fake mustache, so I ran to the bathroom and attached it to my upper lip. I used lots of glue because I didn't know whether I'd end up in the water that day.

Now I was *really* going to be late if I didn't get going. I knew it looked uncool as hell, but I ran all the way to Lisa's house. The thorns on the rose scratched me up a bit, but it didn't matter. I just worried that I'd wreck the rose running that way. I also worried about working up a sweat and stinking around Lisa. I tried to remember whether I'd put on any deodorant that morning but couldn't.

I got to Lisa's a little late, I have to admit, but all the cars were still in the garage, so I guessed they hadn't yet left. It looked like everyone was in the house, probably including Paul. I hadn't seen him in the apartment that morning, so he must have left before I even woke up. Sure enough, Paul—or perhaps I should say *Paula*—was in the house. A thought came to me suddenly; that greasy bastard had the run of the house, while I stood outside like some lousy outcast. I wasn't really as bitter about it as I'm making it sound here, but I'll admit that I felt jealous of "Paula" in there getting ready to go with Lora and Lisa. I wondered whether they took off their clothes in front of him.

I knocked on the back door, and Maria opened it as usual. Speaking Spanish, I asked her to tell everyone I was here, and gave her the card and the flower. "Please give this to Lisa without making a big deal about it," I said. "Try not to let anyone else see it, if you can."

Maria raised her eyebrows and smiled a knowing smile. I figured she owed me a couple of favors and wouldn't mind doing as I asked. About 10 minutes later, everyone came out of the house. Lisa was wearing an oversized tee shirt and sandals, so I didn't get to see her body just yet. Lora looked about the same, and Paula was in some shapeless thing Marty had given her that might be appropriate for the beach if you had a good imagination. I wondered what "she'd" do when everyone stripped off their clothes revealing their swim suits.

We all climbed into the Chrysler. I felt relieved that we weren't going in the limousine. I didn't think Maria could drive it, anyway. We circled the Bay, passed Horny Corner, and headed out towards the Peninsula. We drove all the way to the end of it and had no trouble finding a parking space. In the summer, you usually can't find parking out there to save your life. Lisa didn't say anything about the card and flower. In fact, she didn't speak to me at all, even though I was sitting right beside her. Maybe she was one of those girls who took presents for granted and didn't even bother acknowledging them. Maybe Maria hadn't given them to her. I told myself to stop worrying and just try to have a good time.

It didn't take long to get out of the car. All we had were beach towels and a few toys for the kids. With everyone carrying a little, we were soon on our way. Everyone but Maria's kids who didn't pick up anything and just ran towards the beach. Maria yelled after them, but they didn't have to cross any streets, so I didn't give chase.

A couple of Lisa's and Lora's girlfriends were already sitting on the sand. I guess one twin had called up a few friends and invited them to meet us. These girls were wearing some pretty nice suits and looked fantastic in them. Geese, even Stephanie has a pretty nice body. I guess most girls on the pep squad do.

But I was waiting for Lisa to disrobe. I felt really excited and impatient about this but kept my cool. I noticed Paula wasn't making any efforts to take off his or her smock or whatever you want to call it, so I decided not to rush in disrobing, either. I put my towel down on the sand as quickly as I could without even bothering to unfold it. I wanted to watch Lisa without her knowing I was watching, if you know what I mean. This is a skill all men who like women have to develop eventually if they don't want to be considered perverts. I wondered whether I was any good at it. I don't know. I was wearing the sunglasses they use for snow skiing, the kind where people can't see where your eyes are looking but only their own reflections in the lens. I think they call them mirror sunglasses, and I hoped they would help me out..

I didn't want to miss a thing, so I sat there all cool, pretending to look out over the ocean. Of course, you know that I really never took my eyes off Lisa. I know I go on and on about how good-looking she is, and I don't want to bore you with all the details although I know you'd get all excited looking at Lisa in a bathing suit too unless you're gay or a girl or something. Anyway, Lisa put down her towel and took off most of her clothes, just standing there looking beautiful in her bathing suit. I don't want to get all nasty about this, though I'll admit I was pretty excited in a sexual sense. She really had a terrific body, as I told you before.

And I really liked the suit she had on. It was one of those bikinis popular that summer, a lime-green color called electric green or hot green or florescent green or something like that. It wasn't really that tiny. I mean, I didn't get the impression Lisa was trying to be sexy or anything. She just looked great in that suit and it was sensible, if you know what I mean. Lisa didn't look like the girl in that tiny black French-cut bikini with gold and silver sequins at Horny Corner I told you about. That girl really *was* trying to look sexy, which Lisa wasn't. Somehow, that made me feel even better about her.

By this time, Lora had taken her clothes off, too. She had dressed in a suit exactly like Lisa's except it was that popular florescent pink color I also like. I didn't really check Lora out that much but have to admit that I understand what Paul sees in her. She looks fantastic in a bathing suit and is a nice girl, although she turned me off at first.

Maria's kids were down by the water playing in the surf. Lisa and Lora grabbed a couple of smash ball paddles and a bright yellow rubber ball and headed down towards the harder sand by the water. They didn't say much. They did all this kind of automatically while their girlfriends trailed down to the water behind them, and Paula lumbered about 25 feet behind. I was really relieved they hadn't invited any guys (except me and my brother) along, and neither Lisa nor Lora came across as vixen schemers who were meeting guys on the sly without their parents' permission. I guess they couldn't really do anything bad with Maria there, anyway.

All this left me alone on the beach with Maria. I took off some of my clothes, like the army coat and ski cap and all. At least I would catch some rays, I figured, even though I had a natural tan like my father's. My real motive was to watch the girls from a safe distance. I noticed Maria was mainly watching her kids. I think she's really an excellent mother.

After I'd taken off all my clothes but the swimsuit, Maria looked at me a minute and said in Spanish, "So that's what you look like under all those gardener's clothes. I wondered what you'd look like."

Since she didn't say whether she liked what she saw, I wondered what she meant, but didn't ask because she was a married woman and I didn't want to get into an uncomfortable situation. Besides, I had other things to discuss with her.

"Thanks for giving Lora my present," I said. "Did you have any trouble with it?" What I really wanted to know, of course, was whether Laura had actually received it.

"No trouble at all," Maria said.

I wondered why Lisa hadn't said anything about the card and flower and had even seemed to ignore me in the car. By then, Lora was playing smash ball with Paula, and it really looked funny seeing that big old bugger in a moo-moo trying to hit back the ball while trying to keep his wig from falling off. I really felt like laughing but stifled it. Instead, I smiled inside to avoid having to explain anything to Maria. Lisa was in the water playing with the kids, actually picking them up and throwing them back down. I could see that her hair was wet, and she didn't seem to mind ducking underwater herself. I don't know why, but that really impressed me. I put aside my fear that I had turned off Lisa and would never hear from her again. Instead, I resolved to think positively, as if nothing had happened, and ask Maria about something I'd had on my mind for some time.

"Maria," I said, "I want to be very honest with you about a problem I'm having right now, and I hope you'll understand. I really like Lisa a lot, and don't know what to do about it. Did you mind giving her that present this morning?"

"Not at all," Maria said, grinning. "You seem like a nice young man."

"It's been very hard for me," I continued, "because Lisa's parents watch her like a hawk and don't let her go out with anyone. And besides, they probably see me as a poor little Mexican boy who's not in her league at all."

Maria paused before responding. "I wouldn't worry about it," she said finally. "I believe, someday soon, Mr. Hudson will let his daughters act like normal girls. As for your being poor, well, the Hudsons are really nice people, even though they're rich as can be."

She paused again. "You know," Maria went on, "there's always a place for poor people very near the hearts of rich people when the rich ones are good, like the Hudsons." Then she told me about how kind they'd been to her family and how much they'd done. It was obvious she felt indebted to the whole Hudson family.

When she'd finished, I asked if she would mind helping me out a bit in my effort to get close to Lisa. "I don't have any bad motives," I said. "I'll keep working in the garden until Lisa can go out, and then I'll do everything completely legitimate. I promise not to get any of you in trouble.:"

She laughed good-naturedly, kind of world-wise, if you know what I mean, and said not to worry about getting her in trouble and that she would help me in any way she could.

Just then, a group of kids came up—several of them guys—from the direction of the water. Lisa, Lora, Stephanie and Paula were with them and I vaguely recognized some guys from school. They were surfers, but I didn't really know them because that's not what I am. I don't like their music and none of them are into sports or anything unless you think of surfing as a sport.

Apparently, the guys were friends of Lisa and Lora's, though I don't think they knew them too well. Still, they were looking at me with strange, expectant smiles on their faces. "I told them you'd try out one of their boards," Lisa said, and I swear she almost winked. It wasn't a mocking wink, more like a teasing, knowing wink that made my stomach feel all light and stuff.

Suddenly Maria's kids, coming up behind everyone else, chimed in. "Please, please," they begged. They obviously wanted to see Manuel on a surfboard and wouldn't give up, just like the day I got all wet messing around with that stupid "Alligator Alley" toy. And the kids weren't alone; everyone was urging me on, not only Lisa but Lora, Stephanie and even my brother. The guys weren't mean or anything. They were just putting the pressure on in a friendly way because I guess they imagined I'd never been on a surfboard, which, of course, was true.

I resisted for a while, saying I didn't know how to surf and feared drowning, but everyone just kept at it, including the girls. One guy said he would lend me his board, and another guy about my size said he'd be glad to let me use his wetsuit.

It didn't look like they'd stop until I tried it, so I finally said OK. Everyone seemed excited to hear that. Then one guy I'd seen at school volunteered to give me what he called "the fundamentals." It surprised me how much you have to consider when surfing, just like in football or baseball.

Anyway, I put on the guy's wetsuit. That was an arduous task, which must have taken 10 minutes. I couldn't seem to get it up high enough, and the crotch hung down while the part that held tight around my ankles just didn't want to move up. Lisa took it upon herself to help, laughing as she did. She tugged at the part around my ankles which, after a great deal of effort, moved up an inch or two. Finally, the suit distributed itself more comfortably around my body and I breathed more freely again. To tell the truth, it was a bit too small. And that's when Lisa noticed that the real problem lay in the crotch area, which was way too tight. Without being asked, she started tugging on it. Dangerously close to my --- well, you know what I'm talking about. I don't think she really knew what she was doing. She just wanted to get that damn suit all the way on me, the way it was supposed to be. Lisa was serious now and tugging like crazy. I could see she was really concentrating hard, with her tongue sticking out from the side of her mouth.

"All right, Lisa," I said, "why don't you let me do it myself?" I was afraid something embarrassing would happen, if you know what I mean. I don't want to be any more specific. I think everyone but Lisa knew what could happen because they all were laughing like crazy now, and when I backed away so she couldn't get at my crotch she seemed to get the point and said, "Oh no!" laughing and blushing like crazy. It was a wonderful group of people. Nobody seemed tough or hostile or anything; they were just having good-natured fun.

Finally, the suit seemed to be on as well as it was going to get on, so they put the leg strap around my right ankle. Then they fastened it to the surfboard to keep me from losing it. I wasn't sure whether I liked that, but they assured me I would really tire of swimming after that board every time it got lost. As a beginner, they said, I would truly appreciate that leash.

I don't know why, but I thought this whole surfing thing would really be easy. It looked that way, watching everyone else do it, and I'd never thought of surfing as a tough sport. I picked up the board and ran down to the water, trying to make a good show of it. They called the board a "long board" because it was a couple of inches over nine feet, and the wetsuit I was wearing looked very cool because they had decorated it with many bright colors. The surfers said every suit is a little different, so people on the beach know who they're watching.

I felt absolutely no fear. I was an excellent swimmer, though not exactly an expert. When I actually got into the water, though, I sank down to my chest right away. Now the waves seemed a lot bigger than they had before. And it seemed like all I could see were those huge swells coming at me with white water frothing out everywhere.

Nothing to it, I thought. Easy as pie. I jumped onto the board, hitting it so hard that I fell right off. Bouncing back to the surface, I realized the leash was all wrapped around my other leg. I tried to getting back on the board, this time a bit more lightly. What I forgot, though, was to unwrap the leash on my left leg. I knew I wasn't riding the board correctly because it felt uncomfortable and was wobbling. The front end was sticking way up out of the water. Just about then, a wave of major proportions broke, the white water coming at me with genuine power. I remembered one surfer telling me to go under an oncoming wave but didn't think I needed to because there wasn't enough time, or maybe I didn't even think about it because, well, I didn't try going under.

And that's when the darn thing got me, but good. The nose of the board came back at me so fast I couldn't do a thing. It slapped me so hard on the forehead that I couldn't believe it! Nothing had ever hit me that hard, not even in a fight or on the football field. It was like Manny Pacquiao hit me or something. I thought I'd get knocked out and drown right there with all those guys and girls laughing at me from the beach. Well, I didn't get knocked out or drown, as you can see, but wondered right then how I could get hit so hard in the head and still be conscious. I'm not sure I thought about all this while it was happening because everything went so fast. I probably didn't have time to think much at all.

But the knock on the head was nothing compared to what happened next. The board just took off on its own, leaving me underwater, wondering if I hadn't really lost consciousness after all. Then it came to the surface, shooting up like a great enormous whale. I didn't see it, of course, because I was still underwater, but they told me about it later when I finally made it back to the beach. And because I hadn't untangled the leash from my left foot, the shooting board yanked on it so hard I thought that leg would come off. The bang on the head was hard and all, but it didn't hurt anything like this thing with the leash. I mean, for a minute, I actually thought I'd lost my foot or something.

When I finally came up for air, things seemed a little calmer for a minute. By that I mean the waves weren't breaking on me just then, though there was still lots of noise as they broke all around me. I felt for my left foot and was glad to discover it was still there. I sort of stuck it out of the water and saw that it looked all red and twisted.. Then, looking up at the beach, I noticed all the kids jumping around, waving their hands, shouting and laughing at me.

Suddenly another gigantic wave hit, turning me over and over underwater. I was afraid the board would come up from some place and hit me again. I don't know if you can imagine this, but it felt like being in some great big goddam washing machine with lots of suds and one of my legs tied to the agitator. Anyway, the board didn't hit me and after a minute the agitation stopped. By now, I was close to the shore and really wanted to just grab the board and go in. But I looked up again at everybody on the beach and knew I had really screwed up. To give up now would be as embarrassing as hell.

And then something strange happened. Suddenly there were no waves, and everything seemed as glassy as a shining tabletop. I grabbed my board and pulled myself onto it, moving forward a bit this time so the nose wouldn't stick up so high. Before any more waves could come in, I paddled out as fast as I could. I admit to feeling pretty excited, but also kind of scared.

By this time, I was doing pretty well. I think a little riptide was helping me get out. Suddenly, an enormous wave appeared I hadn't seen before. I feared getting knocked around again and ending back near the shore. Then I remembered to go under. I felt all panicky again but tried to control myself and do what needed to be done. I slid off the board, grabbed it near the nose, flipped over and tried sinking into the water as far as I could. The wave rumbled over my head. Hey, this is easy, I thought! It took me a while to get back on the board because by now I was in pretty deep water.

I tried situating myself just right in anticipation of the next big wave, but this time things didn't go so well. It felt like the wave picked both me and the board up and pushed us back towards the beach. Once again I went under, and this time came up choking and sputtering. I remember wondering whether it was all right to drink sea water, what with all the pollution and everything. Anyway, I really felt like giving up this time. A minute earlier, I'd thought I was getting the hang of it, but now I could see that it didn't always go the same way out here. In fact, if this was what surfing was about, it wasn't very much fun at all. And that's when I realized someone could actually drown out here. I'm not kidding. I wondered if Paul was up on the beach, all concerned about me. I wondered if I seemed to be in real danger or just looked stupid to them. It never looked like other guys had this much trouble getting out, but I have to admit that I'd never really watched them closely, either.

I was just about to give up and go in when another vast wave came up. This time, I did better than the first time. I felt encouraged and tried to get back on the board as fast as I could to keep paddling out. I could feel the slight tug of the riptide carrying me along. Then a monstrous wave started forming, and I feared it would break on me. But it kept on forming and didn't break, so I paddled like hell and just made it over the top before hearing it come crashing down behind me. I remember thanking God about two or three times.

Then everything turned calm again. There were no waves in sight. I paddled like crazy to get well beyond the break line while I could. But it didn't feel like I was moving. I hate to admit it, but I was tired as hell. Honestly, I felt like just putting my head down on the board and lying there without moving, letting the board drift where it wanted. I mean, honestly, it had never seemed to me like surfers were very manly guys. They all looked skinny, with no muscles. Most of them have long hair, though not as many now as used to. I've even seen some guys out there who are old, like over 30 or even 40, and they're not very strong or anything. But these surfers must have tapped into an energy source that I'm not tapped into because right then out in the water I felt more worn out than I think I've ever felt before, even after a track meet or football game. My arms felt like dead weights and, I swear, I was just about to say to hell with it. But then, suddenly, some pretty enormous waves came up, and I could see that I could make it over them if I stroked really hard.

If I stayed where I was, they'd break on me. There was no doubt about that.

Somehow, I got a spurt of energy because I moved my dead-weight arms again and paddled like hell. I remember saying over and over, "Jesus, if you help me this time, I'll try to be a good guy for the rest of my life." I said it over and over to myself, like a prayer or a chant. Anyway, I got over all the waves and realized I was pretty far out now. The people on the beach looked tiny and didn't seem to jump up and down anymore. In fact, it looked like some of them had lost interest in me and were sitting together in little groups, talking and not even looking in my direction. Only a few were looking at me, especially one in a glow-green suit. It was Lisa.

It seemed pretty safe now, being so far out. I said a brief prayer, thanking Jesus for his help, even though I'm not one to say prayers very much. I was still exhausted, believe me, and wondered what I was supposed to do now. Guess I'll try to catch a wave, I thought, and some were coming up behind me just then. I was having difficulty sitting on the board with my legs straddling it like a horse. The board kept moving from side to side, and I was afraid I'd fall off.

A fresh wave was on its way, and suddenly I felt excited again. I lay down on the board and felt glad when it stopped rocking. Despite feeling tired, I paddled as fast as I could, this time towards the beach. As the wave passed under me, not breaking, I rose to the top of it, and looked down its face, a steep blue-green glassy ramp some 20 feet high. It scared the hell out of me, and I prayed to Jesus again that the wave wouldn't pick me up because if it did, I wasn't sure what I would do. I paddled out a little further to where I thought I was before and sat on the rocking board wondering what to do now. Before, I'd been afraid I'd never get out far enough, and now I felt scared that I couldn't get in.

A couple of other gigantic waves came along, and I made some half-hearted efforts to catch them, but was glad when I didn't. And then some smaller waves came up, and now I really wanted to catch one but was too tired to do it. I tried again and again, but it was just too much. I thought if I got in a little closer to the shore, maybe I could catch one.

And then I saw a wave coming along that wasn't exactly huge but was just a little bigger than the little ones I'd been trying so hard to catch.

It broke all around me. I felt smothered by white water but was still on the board as the wave carried me rapidly back towards the shore. Hanging on tight, I remembered what I was supposed to do. I could see ahead a little—my head was above the surface—but there was white water everywhere. I tried standing up, but the foam swept over me. The board was jumping all over the place and spun to the right. Now I was standing up, with the board moving under me as if it had a mind of its own. Wow, I thought, I'm surfing! I was riding the face of a swell, just like the other guys I'd seen. The wave seemed smaller than it had looked from the white water. But I was riding it, anyway. I don't think I'd ever felt so excited!

And I didn't feel tired anymore either. When the ride ended, I didn't even look up, just jumped back on the board and started working my way out again. The ocean was calmer now, and I only had to go under one or two waves to get far enough out. I felt great, on top of the world! I was a surfer, and it was really fun! Maybe if I stuck with it, I could get good like some of the other guys I'd seen.

But then I got worried. Did I still have my mustache on? I checked to make sure it was there. Thank God I'd used lots of glue in the morning. Suddenly, I saw a gigantic wave coming. I'd thought I was out far enough but could see now that if I stayed where I was, the wave would break on me. I started paddling out, thinking I could get over the wave. But it was too late; the wave broke, throwing me and the board down to its foot. This time my nose hit the board so hard I thought someone had punched me. The wave rolled me and the board over and over. When I regained control, I felt my nose to see if it had broken. Guys in fights and in football had hit me pretty hard before, but never like this. But my nose felt intact, even though bloody. I figured I'd better get out of the water before some sharks came along and attacked me. And then, to make matters worse, I realized my mustache was gone! Jesus, I thought, what now?

I got on the board, paddled out a bit, and sat there in confusion and despair. But then a plan began developing in my mind. Maybe if I sat out there long enough, all the kids would go home, and never notice my mustache had disappeared. I wasn't sure, though, that the owners of the wetsuit and surfboard would leave without them. Heck, maybe they'd even paddle out to get me.

Then it occurred to me I could use the bloody nose to my advantage. I'd just hold my nose when I got in and not let anyone mess with it. Then no one would see that my mustache was gone. Great idea, but how would I get in? I knew I could ride the white water on my belly without having to stand up or anything. I would hold on to my nose all the way and then leave. Then I'd just sit there all afternoon holding my nose while everyone else laughed and talked and had a good time. I'd hang on to my nose until they took me back to Lisa's house, then I'd go on home holding my nose until I was too far away for anyone to see.

Suddenly, a gigantic wave came along. It looked like it would break before I caught it, perfectly in sync with my plan. But it didn't break. It picked me up, all the way to the top. Once again, I looked 20 feet down on its glassy surface, but this time I wasn't so scared. To hell with the plan, I stood up easily as you can imagine and, God, was I excited! Suddenly, the board slid right down to the bottom of the wave with me still on it, and its nose dove right into the water. Now the wave had me in its clutches. Jesus, I hated this! I was so mad I didn't even care if the board jumped up, knocked me in the head, and I drowned. I swear to God I was done.

But the board didn't hit me. Instead, it carried me even closer to the shore; so close, in fact, that I could hear the voices of my friends. They were standing in a group on the beach, watching. And there was Lisa in the water actually swimming in my direction! I grabbed my nose, which was still bleeding, and cupped it in my hand. I didn't think she, or anybody, had yet noticed the missing mustache. I braced myself for her arrival, which was imminent.

"Hey, are you OK?" Lisa asked. "What's wrong with your nose?"

"Oh, no big deal," I said, "just kinda smashed it on the board." I'm sure she could see the blood dripping down. I was also sure she wanted to look, but firmly held my ground. "Don't worry," I reassured her, holding my nose even tighter. "It will be just fine."

"Too proud to show me?" she inquired, rather teasingly, I thought. That's when it occurred to me that an enormous wave could come along and blow my cover. "Can you help me in?" I asked. "We should probably get out of the water as soon as we can."

I could tell Lisa was more worried about my nose than she was about getting clunked on the head by a surfboard, but she said no more as we slowly made our way in with me still holding onto my nose.

The guys and girls on the shore also wanted to know what had happened. I told them the board hit me, but I may have also banged my nose on a rock or something. Everybody started making a fuss over me, wanting to see my nose to wipe off the blood. I've never seen so many future doctors and nurses. Still, I didn't let any of them touch my face, not even Lisa. I tried to joke about how now I knew what surfing was all about, acting as cool as I could. Then Maria dug into her purse and came up with all kinds of tissues. I took them with my free hand, keeping the other one tight on my nose. I wiped myself off as best as I could with one hand. Meanwhile, the kids were trying to unchain me from the surfboard and take off the wetsuit. They succeeded in both efforts without noticing that my mustache was gone.

As I've said before, this was really a bunch of nice kids. Even though they were rich. I know most surfers have lots of money because they buy all kinds of surfing equipment and fancy clothes that cost a lot. They also have plenty of time to surf. I don't think any of these guys have to work at summer jobs like so many other young people do just to keep themselves afloat in the real world and not the ocean. But these kids were really nice, if you know what I mean. They seemed to care more about me than they did about the equipment or the wetsuit. I knew that because they didn't even say anything about the great big glass shatter on the surfboard where my head had hit or a couple of little tears in the suit. They just acted like they really cared for me, even if they saw me as some kind of poor, migrant Mexican farm worker or something.

They even plied me with compliments regarding my surfing ability, especially as it was my first time. I knew I'd really screwed up out there and had even twice been in danger. I got one really wonderful ride, though, and was proud of that! It surprised me to learn that the waves were only four or five feet that day. I'd thought they were a lot bigger. I guess you measure the waves from the back instead of the front, or something like that.

But I must tell you I've developed a healthy respect for surfing. I know now that it's a real sport that requires lots of skill. I knew football takes lots of skill and can be very dangerous, but now I knew that to be true of surfing too. You don't hear much about it, but I'll bet people get killed surfing, especially in places like Hawaii. I even have some sense now of how thrilling it can be, but that doesn't mean I want to try it again anytime soon. In fact, I doubt that I'll ever try it again, at all. If I never see another surfboard in my life, I assure you, that will be just fine.

Later, Paul told me he was worried while I was out there surfing, or whatever I was doing out there. Twice he thought about blowing his whole disguise by stripping down to his underwear, bra, and pantyhose to jump in and save me. But I kept on coming up for air, he said, which made him think I was ok. Especially when I kept going out for more. A couple of times he even had to reassure some guys who wanted to go in for me that everything would be ok and, sure enough, that's how it finally turned out. I was glad now that nobody, especially Paul, had come in to save me. The entire experience was a lesson in life, really, and I'm glad I got through it all by myself. I would have felt embarrassed if anyone had come out to save me. I never would have forgiven myself had I blown things for Paul. And what would everyone say had I come up without my mustache? What would *I* have said?

The kids finally started losing interest in helping me with my nose, even Lisa. They could see that I wasn't going to let them. I told them they could go on and have a good time and just forget about me and I'd just take care of myself. I was trying to be a good old guy about everything by cutting up and joking and all. But I knew I wasn't exactly bringing it off. Try entertaining people sometime with your hand over your mouth or your finger in your ear or up your nose or something, and you'll realize it isn't easy. I know people will laugh at you when you put your finger up your nose at first, but just try sitting there joking with them with your finger up your nose for half an hour. I think you'll find that, after a while, you're not too funny.

But Lora and Lisa wouldn't hear of it. They wanted to take me home right away, and so did Maria. I sat beside Lisa on the ride home in the car, holding my nose all the way. The kids kept asking their mother how Manuel's nose was, and Lisa talked to me about her Spanish class and how they were discussing this silly hero called Don Quixote or somebody like that who got into all kinds of trouble and did stupid things with his pal called Sancho Panza. But this Quixote guy had nobility of spirit and didn't give up on anything until he died. She seemed to be talking to herself more than to me. She didn't look at me very much, probably because she didn't enjoy seeing me sitting there holding my nose with a bloody tissue all over my face. Anyway, I remember she said they had made this Don Quixote story into some kind of play or something, maybe even a musical, and that she loved the music in it. I don't remember what she said very well. I was too self-conscious about how stupid I must have looked sitting there all dressed up like a migrant farm worker with a bloody nose. I was sitting beside the girl of my dreams, loving her more and more by the minute, but feeling like the most repulsive guy in the world and as stupid as hell. I want to ask you whether you can imagine how bad I felt sitting there like that? I mean can you even imagine it? All I wanted was to get to where we were going as soon as possible and get home. Maybe everything would be OK in the morning. I didn't know.

Finally, we got to their house, and I wanted to get out of the car as fast as I could. I felt so embarrassed I thought I was going to break out crying. All this seemed so impossible. I didn't even care what Paula did with himself. He seemed to make out well on his own. I almost bolted down the street. I felt tears welling up in my eyes and wanted to get home right away. Maybe I'd feel better after I'd taken a shower. I wasn't sure.

But then I heard Lisa calling after me. I really didn't want to be around her just then. But I stopped and turned anyway, just in time to see her running up to me. She had my beach towel. I must have taken off without it. "I hope your nose is all right," she said. "I'm really sorry I made you go out on that surfboard just because everyone wanted you to. I didn't know you'd get hurt or anything. I hope you can forgive me."

My heart swelled with affection for this sweet girl. "Don't worry," I said, "I've been hit in the nose before. And, anyway, it was really fun."

She smiled. "Well, you did pretty well, and I admire you for not giving up. I don't care whether you can surf; the important thing is trying your best."

I told her I better get going. I felt relieved and didn't feel like crying anymore. But Lisa still wanted to talk and wouldn't let me go.

"You know," she said, "I really want to thank you for the thoughtful gifts you gave me this morning. I enjoyed our talk too. I'll probably send you a card sometime soon. You're a nice guy, and I hope we can be friends for a long time. And I think I'll take your advice and go down to see Michael at the beauty shop sometime next week." She came up and kissed me on the cheek. She didn't even seem to mind how bad I looked just then.

Then she took a few steps backwards and said, "Thanks a lot, Manuel. Please take care of yourself, and I'll see you soon, I hope." She didn't say anything else but turned around and ran off down the sidewalk with her beach thongs scraping the cement all the way until she rounded the corner and disappeared.

I'm not going to bore you with everything I was thinking because I'm not sure my thoughts were very clear, anyway. All I remember was that ever since I'd met Lisa, the surprises just kept coming. I'd almost forgotten about the presents I'd given her that morning, it seemed so long ago. But she hadn't forgotten. This was really some girl.

Chapter Seven

I went right home, took a shower, and felt better like I hoped I would. I looked in the mirror both before and after the shower and discovered that I wasn't as messed up as I thought. I could tell I was going to have two black eyes, though. I could see the skin under them turning purple and knew from experience that both would be big, beautiful, and black by morning. I wondered whether I should go to school with two black eyes. Everybody would think I got into a fight, and I was tiring of telling lies all the time.

I got dressed and sat down at my desk, trying to concentrate on homework. The next day was Monday, and those damn teachers never failed to pile up homework on the weekends. I wondered whether any of those old fogies were ever kids. What were they trying to do to us, drive us crazy? There ought to be a law against these people. Usually, I don't worry much about homework. If I feel like doing it, I do it and if I don't, I don't. Most of the time I couldn't care less. I wish my homework would do itself because it usually doesn't get done. And, anyway, it could probably do itself better than I can do it. But as I told you earlier, my attitude had changed since meeting Lisa. Now I was trying to make myself worthy of hanging out with her. So, I told myself to settle down and try to get something done.

But all I could think about was Lisa and what an unusual girl she was and how much I loved her. She was beautiful and had an impressive body but wasn't all stuck on herself or anything. I really felt cared for after that surfing accident at the beach. And now this girl was planning to come down to have a talk with the guy at the beauty shop. I'm glad he and I are the same person, if you know what I mean. But I'm sure there's no way you could know what I mean, so let me start again. I'm glad that Manuel Ortega and Michael Santos are the same person. Otherwise, I'd be jealous as hell. I admit, though, to feeling a little funny about this. It's hard to explain, but I really want Lisa to love Michael Santos and not Manuel Ortega. But when I'm Manuel Ortega, I feel like I'm falling in love with Lisa as Manuel and am jealous hearing that she's all hung up on Michael Santos. After all, today she kissed Manuel Ortega, not Michael Santos. She didn't even care about all the blood on Manuel's face. Which made me wonder whether Lisa was a two-timer or something. Could she be all tender and loving with one guy while thinking about another one? Suddenly I felt depressed and stopped worrying about it. I can't explain this to you, anyway, it's just all too complicated.

 I was excited about Lisa coming down to see me at the beauty shop, but worried about it, too. I hadn't had much trouble talking to Lisa as Manuel, but wasn't sure how things would turn out as Michael. If Lisa saw me with two black eyes and a haircut like Manuel's, she might put two and two together and I wasn't sure what would happen then. I mean, when you're all hung up on a girl like I was with Lisa, you worry all the time about doing something that will put an end to it. In fact, even when you're crazy about a girl, you worry so much about losing her, you might as well not even have her. I hate admitting this to you. It might even be bad luck to say it, but it's true. One time I liked a girl so much and was so worried about losing her all the time that she dumped me for some other guy. And you know what? In a weird sort of way, I was actually glad she dumped me because then I didn't have to worry about losing her anymore. I know I shouldn't talk this way because it's bad luck, so I'd better change the subject.

 If Lisa was going to come down to the beauty shop, she'd just have to come on down. I'd think of something when she got there. I saw I could think well on my feet these days, but I'd have to be prepared just in case she came by. I decided I'd better not miss school the next day. Maybe I'd wear sunglasses to hide my black eyes, and for football practice, the guys would think I'd put on that black stuff you see athletes wearing under their eyes to cut down on the glare and all.

It was a little after eight p.m., and I wasn't getting anywhere on my homework when someone knocked on my bedroom door. It was Paul, dressed now as himself. "Hey, there's someone on the phone for you," Paul said, waving my cell phone in front of me. I didn't know how he got it. I must have left it in the kitchen, which is much closer to Paul's room than to mine. It really annoyed me, though, that he'd answered my phone instead of just bringing it to me.

"Who is it?" I asked, shielding my voice with one hand while grabbing the phone with the other.

"Lisa," Paul said and, without another word, turned and marched back into his room.

When Paul got down to his homework on Sunday nights, he was like a fanatic, working until midnight, one, or even two in the morning and refusing to talk to a soul. I think if the house blew up or there was a major earthquake and it tumbled down around his ears, he would just keep on working. Which is why it surprised me he'd stop to answer my phone.

I'll let you in on a secret; for the past few days, I've been looking for a word to describe how I'm feeling about certain things. You know, like when you have mixed emotions? Like wanting it and not wanting it at the same time or loving something and hating it all at once. I knew there was a word for that but wasn't sure what it was. I think I'd heard about it in English class or somewhere. Anyway, I found the word in the dictionary the other day. It took me a long time because I had to look at every word in the dictionary starting with "A" until I found it. I guess you could say I really wanted to know that word. I was lucky because it starts with "A." Thank God it didn't start with a "U" or a "V" because then it would have taken me hours. The word is "ambivalent," which means what I told you earlier. I looked it up in two dictionaries because the first one didn't give a very good definition, but the second one convinced me it was the word I was looking for.

I'll use the word right now. I really felt ambivalent about getting a call from Lisa just then. How in the world had she gotten my number, and did she want to talk to Manuel or Michael? I wanted to ask Paul, but he was already gone, and it would have been rude to keep Lisa hanging on forever. Part of me really wanted to talk to her. By now my heart beat like mad and I felt crazy happy. I didn't know what to expect—maybe she had found out about everything and was calling to tell me I was a jerk who she never wanted to see again. That last thought terrified me, and I felt an insane impulse to run outside and get as far away from that phone as I could. Good old Paul would eventually discover my phone on the floor, pick it up and, if Lisa was still on the line, tell her I wasn't home, which would not be a lie. He could make up some sort of excuse or explanation. He knew more about what was going on than I did, anyway.

I knew I would have to man up and pick up the phone. I decided not to be the first to say who it was. Maybe she'd give some sort of clue. I'd play it really cool until I knew what was going on.

I picked up the phone and said, "Hey Lisa, how are you? Sorry to keep you waiting. I was deep into some math homework. I'm really sorry."

Her next words solved the mystery immediately.

"I really know what you mean, Manuel," she said. "I've got a lot of homework myself and will probably be up all night. I really shouldn't have gone to the beach today, but the weather's been so great that I've had spring fever. I wanted to check up on that nose of yours. How is it, and how are you doing?"

I told her I was doing fine and thanked her for calling. I felt relieved but wanted to know how she got my phone number. Not that I meant to take it away from her or anything.

"I didn't know you had my number, Lisa."

"Ha!" she laughed that sweet laugh of hers. "You forgot you filled out a job application here."

I couldn't even remember writing my phone number on that application. I don't think I ever even finished it. But now I felt glad I hadn't given them a fake number. At least I thought I felt that way. Anyway, Lisa said she had to go and just wanted to know how I was doing.

"Oh, and one other thing," she said. "Who was that who answered the phone? The voice sounded familiar."

I felt my chest tightening in panic but told her it was just my little brother. I said his name was "Pedro" or "Pancho" or something like that. I don't remember exactly what I said because I wanted to drop the subject as fast as I could. It was really bothering me to be lying to her as much as I was. I was making myself sick, I truly was.

After she hung up, I went back to my room. What a close call. It was about 8:30 p.m., and I thought I'd like to hear some music. I turned on the stereo and tried to lose myself in the sounds. I couldn't believe how complicated everything was getting. Turning on the music was the best thing I could do. The rhythm of it drew me in, making my troubles disappear. I felt sleepy, perhaps more than I ever had before. I said to myself, "To hell with homework. Maybe the fairies will do it overnight." The thought made me chuckle because I really try to act cool, even while being the world's corniest S.O.B. I turned out the light and slid into bed without even undressing, getting into my pajamas or brushing my teeth. I went right to sleep, and don't remember a thing after that. I don't even remember dreaming.

Chapter Eight

I went to school on Monday wearing sunglasses. No one bugged me about my black eyes. After getting up that morning, I'd noticed they weren't as black and blue as I'd feared. There was no doubt I had two black eyes, just not as bad as they could have been. After school, I kept looking for Lisa to show up at the beauty shop, but she didn't come in. I was sort of hoping she'd come by Tuesday because I'd made a lot of preparations. I don't need to tell you what they were because I don't want to bore you, but she didn't come in on Tuesday either. I started thinking she'd decided not to come after all and felt depressed.

On Wednesday, things got really busy. Some of Lisa's and Lora's friends had come in early, and then later there was a lull. I sort of dressed up on Wednesday, thinking it was now or never. Lisa would either come in today, or not at all. At least that's what I kept telling myself to keep from getting depressed even more. I had the sunglasses on; you know the kind you wear to the beach when you don't want anyone to see your eyes. I still had black eyes, but they were already clearing up. A little black Russian-looking cap rested on my head so that Lisa, if she came in, wouldn't notice I had the same haircut as Manuel. I was alone in the shop, lost in my own thoughts, when she finally walked through the door.

God was she beautiful! I felt so close to her at that moment that I wanted to run over and kiss the daylights out of her, but then remembered that I was Michael Santos now and not Manuel Ortega. I wasn't supposed to know this girl well enough to attack her.

"Hi there," I said. "My name's Michael. Do you have an appointment?"

"No, Michael," she said, smiling, "I don't. I can come back another time if I need one."

The idea of her turning around and marching back out the door broke my heart so much that I felt like crying. I'm sure glad I didn't though.

"It shouldn't be a problem," I said, trying to sound casual. "We're not too busy right now. In fact, I'm the only one here because Wednesday afternoons are _never_ too busy. Tell me your name and I'll put it right down in the appointment book as if you'd had an appointment all along."

"Lisa," she said, smiling even more broadly. "My name is Lisa Hudson." She spelled out the last name. So far, so good, I thought.

I wasn't really supposed to be working there unsupervised, but a friend from the west side of town had made me a fake hairdresser's license. The owner of the shop knew about it but didn't really mind. He knew I was pretty good at cutting hair and enjoyed doing it. He also knew I was reliable.

Telling a customer your name and asking for hers was routine in this beauty shop. We tried to be cool here. We tried to establish a first-name relationship with every customer. We didn't call them Mr. or Mrs. So-and-so like you hear in other places. We even called old ladies by their first names and put down those names in the appointment book like "Ronald at 2:00 p.m." or "Mary at 9:00 a.m." The owner thinks this really makes a good impression so customers will consider us very relaxed and "with it" or some such thing.

I must admit, it's really a great place to work. The shop has a kind of sexy atmosphere with the wallpaper all done up in the sort of colors you might see at a bordello or something. There's lots of silver, like on the light fixtures and such. There's even a part of the wall that has silver wallpaper. The decorators covered the chairs and an enormous sofa in black leather. The customers can really relax on that couch because it's so soft and sleek that you want to sink down into it, which most of them do. There are magazines all over the black plastic-and-glass coffee table, like US News and World Report and Cosmopolitan and about the economy and business and photography and all. There are also magazines like Fitness and Self and so on; I really enjoy looking at these magazines myself, even though some of them are really women's magazines. I enjoy looking at the girls in them and reading about what women are up to these days.

The truth is that men like coming in here as much as women do. I think the men really like the sexiness of the place because the girls working here dress in sexy low-cut tops and wear their hair like prostitutes used to in the old days, all frizzy and unkempt looking like they just got out of bed or something.

The music we play, lots of punk and soul and rock and stuff, enhances the sexiness. We don't play it too loud, though, in consideration of our older customers. In fact, they seem to like it even more than the kids do. I really get off when I see some old lady with wet hair tapping her foot in time to the music. I can just imagine her getting up out of that beauty chair with her apron and dancing all over the place like you see in the movies. The music really fits the place, and nobody seems to mind it.

Oh yes, and I'm supposed to look really "now" too. I'm even supposed to play up the idea that I might be homosexual or something. Women don't mind that at all. In fact, they seem more comfortable with a gay-looking guy doing their hair. I guess when it comes right down to it, a hairdresser gets kind of intimate with his clients. I mean, he washes their hair and rubs their scalp and even massages their shoulders while doing their nails and shaving their necks. Sometimes he might even work on their feet. I guess they feel more comfortable knowing the guy's not going to come on to them. I guess they want to save that for their husbands or boyfriends or whatever, I don't know. I don't think I'll ever really understand women. Can you imagine a man going somewhere where they cut his hair and rub their hands all over him, wanting a lesbian to do it instead of a good-looking straight girl? That seems ridiculous to me. But I guess I'm a man who will never see things the way girls do. It seems like women don't mind being around gay guys at all. In fact, some girls will only hang around gay guys and won't even go out with a guy who's straight. I read somewhere that they're called "fruit flies." I don't dislike lesbians. It's just that I wouldn't be around a bunch of them. I'm sure I'd feel stupid and useless if I did. Like I said, I have nothing against lesbians but can't help thinking it's sad finding out a girl's a lesbian, especially when she's hot.

I led Lisa to the back of the room, put one of the plastic aprons on her, and asked her to sit down in one of the beauty chairs next to the sink. "Scoot back a bit and lean *way* back," I instructed. I got her hair all wet, put some shampoo on it, and started lathering. I was truly enjoying myself. God, it felt good to be touching this girl! I tried to keep my feelings from being too obvious. I knew I was spending an extra-long time lathering her hair, but I really didn't care. Her hair was long, blond and beautiful and I loved it like crazy!

Finally, the shampooing was done, so I dried her hair and placed a towel over her shoulders. Then we walked together to the chair at my station, and I adjusted it to work on her comfortably. I asked how she wanted her hair done, and her answer really floored me.

"Cut it short," she said. "Punk style, close around the sides and in back with about three inches left on top."

I couldn't believe what I was hearing. Cutting off all that hair was simply unimaginable. "That would be a tragedy," I blurted, without even thinking. "Your hair looks beautiful the way it is. Why don't we just cut off a couple of inches of split ends and leave it at that? And anyway, the punk look is way out of style."

"No," she insisted without a second's pause, "I want it short."

And so I steeled myself and pulled out the scissors. As I began cutting, my heart felt broken. I've seen movies where some woman cuts off her hair. Maybe she cuts it off to sell because she has some starving kid at home or has to assume a disguise or something like that. And when she's cutting off her own hair, or someone else is doing it, she cries, but they cut it off, anyway. And usually there's a sad scene where all you see is the amputated hair slowly falling to the ground.

For the second time that day, I almost wanted to cry. Can you imagine a hairdresser doing that? But she didn't seem to notice. The one thing I refused to do, though, was allow all that beautiful hair to fall to the ground. I don't think I let a single strand from her head end up on the floor. Instead, I lovingly placed it all on the shelf in front of the mirror at my station. I was sure she'd want to take it home.

Then I noticed she didn't look half bad with most of her hair gone.

This was especially obvious after I dried what I'd left on her head with the dryer. She had a nice-shaped head, like my mother said I had. And her face was so pretty that it stood out even more now that most of her hair was gone. Suddenly, I didn't feel like crying anymore. Who cared if the cut might be a little out of style? It looked great on her! When I'd finished cutting, I made sure there weren't any hairs left on her shoulders or clothes or anywhere. I thought about massaging her shoulders but decided not to. Instead, I noticed she had a yellow tank top on and wasn't wearing a bra. So I leaned over to see if I could look down the front of her shirt. Unfortunately, I leaned over so far that my sunglasses fell off into her lap. She looked right up into my face, me standing there embarrassed as hell with two black eyes, probably blushing like crazy. Obviously, she knew I was trying to look down the front of her tank top, but she didn't seem to mind at all. She just smiled a warm and beautiful smile, handed back the sunglasses, and paid me with a five-dollar tip,

"See you later," she said, and was about to leave.

Suddenly I remembered the disembodied hair on the counter. "Hey, don't you want to take this with you?" I asked.

She looked at me quizzically, as if the question was odd. "I'm not into saving things like that, Michael," she said. "You can just throw it away. If I evert want hair, I'll just grow some more."

She smiled at me again—not unfriendly—and turned to go.

Later I gathered up all her hair, wrapped it in a piece of white paper and took it home to put in a nice clean shoebox in my closet. I'd really be mad if you thought I did anything nasty with that hair. Just get any thoughts like that out of your mind right now. Her hair sits in the box on a shelf of the bookcase in my room. I've put it in nicer white tissue paper. I threw away the paper in which I originally brought it home. Occasionally, I take the box off the shelf and look at Lisa's hair, but never touch it because I don't want to get it dirty.

Back at the beauty shop, Lisa seemed in a hurry to get away.. She was already out the door, rushing down the sidewalk, when something else occurred to me. I hustled outside as fast as I could and called after her. "Hey Lisa," I yelled. She paused and turned around. "Who do you have for fifth period? What class is it?"

She told me she was taking Spanish with Mr. Perez for fifth period, without even asking why I wanted to know. Then she said, "Bye, Michael, see you later," and disappeared.

I walked back into the beauty shop. Nobody was there, so I went over to the phone. Lisa would be a little late for sixth period, but it was fifth period, the one she'd skipped to have her hair done, that worried me. I didn't want her getting into trouble. I didn't know whether she had a plan of her own but wanted to be as careful as possible.

I called the school and some student office helper answered. I told her my name was Mr. Santos, and I had to talk to Paul Santos right away. It was an emergency. She asked about two or three times who I was and who I wanted to talk to and why I was calling. I felt glad this wasn't a genuine emergency! Another girl got on the phone. I'm pretty sure she was a student too because she asked all the questions again. Then she transferred me to another phone and this time a woman answered. She couldn't help me either, she said, transferring me to yet someone else. I think I was finally in touch with Paul's counselor, Mrs. Smart, the best one at our school. Her name really was "Smart," I'm not kidding. Anyway, I told her what I'd told all the others, and she seemed concerned. She said Paul would be in her office in a minute or two. She hoped it wasn't too serious. I didn't want to offer a long explanation but told her it was an emergency having to do with Paul's football uniform and wasn't a life-and-death situation or anything like that. I'd been on hold for maybe five minutes, when finally Paul picked up the phone.

"What's the matter, Dad? he wanted to know.

"Paul, this is Michael calling from the beauty shop. Try not to let Mrs. Smart know if she's close to the phone."

"OK," he said, "what's up? I have to get back to class. We're having a test." I knew he wasn't in his girl's outfit because it was sixth period.

"Do you remember that evening on the pier when we promised to help each other whenever we could?" I inquired.

"Yeah," he said. "Can you get to the point? I've got to get back."

"Well, Lisa came to have her hair done at the shop today and skipped fifth period to do it. Could you get Mr. Perez' absence list and erase the little pencil dot bubble by her name so she won't get in trouble?"

Paul hesitated a minute. I could tell he was wavering.

"OK," he finally said, "I'll do it for you this time. But this is the last time, got it? Don't ask me again. I gotta go. Is there anything else?"

"No, Paul, that's it," I said. "Thank you. I owe you one."

He said goodbye and hung up.

I knew Paul could pull off things like that. He could hang around the office or teacher's lounge, and nobody would notice or mind. The teachers, administrators, and office staff all knew what a terrific student Paul was, and everyone respected him. I knew I was asking a lot. Paul didn't enjoy breaking rules and messing around. He didn't like abusing the privileges he had. But I hoped this time he would make an exception and help me keep Lisa out of trouble. I was confident he'd do it because he'd said he would.

I kept thinking about it after hanging up. And suddenly I wondered whether I'd made a hit with Lisa in the beauty shop. It seemed like everything had gone smoothly, but it also seemed like a normal conversation with a customer at the salon. Maybe I hadn't made a good impression on her. She probably thought I was the dullest guy in the world. I tried to stop worrying about it and think positively. In fact, I could barely even remember what we'd talked about at the beauty shop that day—probably mostly small talk. I decided it wasn't important.

Chapter Nine

The next Saturday, I got up early and made it to Lisa's by 7:30 a.m.. Nobody seemed to be up yet. I went right to the tool shed to get started and there on the wooden workbench lay an envelope with the name "Manuel" on it. It was the same glow-green color as Lisa's bathing suit the previous weekend. I got all excited and worried at the same time. I carefully opened the envelope, trying not to tear it too much. There was a card inside with a pretty design on the front. Inside of the card, I found a letter addressed to me. Here's what it said:

Dear Manuel,

I am not just writing you this letter because I feel I owe you one, but because I really want to talk to you, and I'm not sure if we will have a chance today or not. I really appreciate the lovely card and rose you gave me last week. I can see you designed the card yourself, and in retrospect your creative abilities. Thank you so much, once again. I followed your advice and went to see Michael Santos at the beauty shop. He is nice and seems very interesting too. I hope I can get to know him much better in the future. You were right about how I should approach a boy directly because I really enjoyed talking to Michael face-to-face. If you have any more suggestions or can help me, please let me know. If you have time today, I'd love to talk. With affection from your friend,

Lisa

I read this letter several times and wasn't sure exactly what to think of it. I was glad Michael Santos hadn't turned Lisa off or anything. I was happy to get the letter, don't get me wrong. But I was getting sick of all this lying. In fact, I was feeling disgusted with myself.

That Friday after school and before the game, I rushed down to the costume shop. I had to get a new mustache because I'd lost the old one surfing like I told you. I had a hard time buying it, though, and not because it was expensive. I just wanted to give up on this disguise and talk to Lisa face-to-face. Lisa had shown herself to be trustworthy, and I wanted to tell her everything as soon as possible. So I decided to tell her the truth the next day. I didn't care what happened. I just wanted her to know everything. I felt up under my nose for the new mustache, grabbed it at the end and pulled it off. Then I threw it in the trash. I knew I still had glue all over my lip, but didn't care. I'd wash my face before seeing her.

The next morning Lisa's place again seemed deserted, so I got right to work. There isn't much of a lawn in their backyard, though the Hudsons have a power mower. I fill just one load in the catcher. That's all the grass there is. Alihandro had already put the plastic trash containers out in a line in front of the house because Saturday afternoon was trash day. When I was done with the lawn, I put the power mower back in the shed, took off the catcher, and started towards the trash area along the street to unload it. The garage door was already open, and I could see Maria coming towards me with a package in her hand. She smiled pleasantly and said, "Good morning, Manuel. How's your nose doing today?"

I experienced a moment of panic, thinking she was alluding to my now-absent mustache, but then relaxed a bit, realizing the subject of her interest was my recent surfing accident. "It's feeling great," I told her. "No problem at all anymore."

"Good," she said, "I'm glad your nose is all right." Then, with no mention of its hairless state, she went on through the garage door and into the house as I continued out towards the trash cans. I wasn't paying attention or thinking about anything, when I noticed Boy Jerome's lowered black Cadillac parked in front of the house. I continued to the trash can, emptied the grass catcher, and tried to get back to the garage without Jerome seeing me. Unfortunately, though, he's an observant guy, had seen me immediately and, what's worse, recognized me for who I really was. I experienced a moment of regret at pulling off that darn phony mustache.

"Hey, Santos, Michael Santos," he shouted out the window of the parked car. "How ya doing? Haven't seen ya in a while; Watcha been up to?"

I looked behind me, hoping we were out of earshot and, much to my relief, saw nobody in the garage or yard. I hated doing it, but walked right up to the car so he would stop shouting.

"Hi, Jerome," I said, "how you doing?" I didn't want to call him "Boy Jerome" or anything, so I just called him "Jerome." You really had to be careful around this guy because he was dangerous, as I told you before.

"So, this is where you're hanging out, old buddy," Jerome went on in this slickest voice. "There are lots of guys down on the west side who'd really like to know where your pad is, if you get my drift."

These guys really make me sick. They can't even talk to you without making what sounds like a threat. All they do is act tough and scare people to death. I wondered whether Jerome would ever grow up. He'd probably be dead before that ever happened. There were rumors that he had killed people himself, or had them killed, or whatever. A guy like this has plenty of enemies.

"Jerome, I don't live here," I said. "I just work here a few hours a week. And I'd really appreciate it if you wouldn't go around telling people you'd seen me here or anything." I was getting mad. I wasn't really in the mood to take threats from a guy like Jerome. I used to put up with lots of crap on the west side of town, but this wasn't the west side, and I hadn't brushed up against someone like Jerome in quite a while. I was feeling madder and madder and resenting this thug sitting in his car in front of Lisa's house.

"You know, Jerome, I imagine that the good people around here would like to find out what kind of business you're in. They'd probably do something about it, too." I knew I was on dangerous ground now. Maybe I'd gone too far. What I'd said had just seemed to pop out of my mouth. I had to work on controlling my anger.

"Hey, boy, you'd better cool that," Jerome said. You're sounding like some fool." He didn't have to explain. He had no trouble calling me "boy" but would get mad as hell if I called him "Boy Jerome" or something like that. I stood my ground.

"You know, Jerome," I said, "you're the guy who started talking about spreading the word around, but I want you to know that what goes around comes around. You know what *I'm* talking about."

That seemed to calm him down. He stopped threatening me, and we dropped the subject. There was something I really wanted to know, though; just who was his customer here? Who had he come to see? Maria, or somebody else? Jerome told me it was a professional secret, of course, but since he knew me from the west side and I'd never given him any reason not to trust me, he could tell me it wasn't Maria. In fact, he said, it was Hudson's "old lady" who was a cokehead and willing to receive his "presents" now and then.

Oh, so it was Mrs. Hudson! I'd always thought there was something funny about her, not that I really knew her or anything. The strange thing was that she almost never was home. She was always off doing something or the other. In fact, I believe I'd only seen her little Mercedes in the garage once.

Jerome and I exchanged a few more pleasantries, and then he drove off. I felt scared as hell of him but didn't want him to know. He was like a shark or grizzly bear and would feed off fear or weakness wherever he found it. Maybe he respected that I stood up to him. I didn't know for sure, but what I knew was that he peddled information and dope, and it surprised me he'd talked about Mrs. Hudson. I wasn't exactly his friend or anything and never bought dope from him, but I knew him from the west side because, well, everybody knows everybody over there.

I thought about Mrs. Hudson and Lisa as I got back to work in their yard. Alihandro had told me the old man wanted some juniper plants dug up and something else planted there instead. Pretty soon it was 12 o'clock, and I was feeling the first pangs of hunger. I had forgotten to bring a lunch of my own. And I wondered whether Lisa would come out and feed me just like she'd done before. Jesus, I was already depending on her, something I'd told myself never to do.

Lisa didn't come out at 12, 12:30 or even at one. She must be busy inside, I told myself. Or maybe she didn't really want to talk to me at all. The hunger swelled inside me, but I just kept my head down and my hands on the hoe.

About two o'clock she finally came out carrying a tray laden with sandwiches, chips, brownies and Coke. She'd baked the brownies herself, she said, and wanted to know my opinion. She had changed the recipe or something and wondered how successful she'd been. She apologized for not coming out sooner, but didn't bother telling me why.

"Thanks for the card," I said. "Anytime you want to write to me is just fine."

I felt like I was treading water talking to her, not going anywhere. I don't even remember what all we said, but I knew I just had to dive right in. We had barely begun eating when I took off my blue-knit cap and told her I had something important to say. "I don't want you to get scared or upset or anything," I said, as gently as I could, "but I'm not really Manuel Ortega. I'm Michael Santos, the guy you met at the beauty shop last Wednesday."

I really didn't know how she would take this. Maybe not very well. Almost immediately, I felt sorry that I'd told her.

But she didn't scream, throw food at me, or run into the house crying. Instead, she brightened right up and gave me a heartwarming smile. She's always radiant, as I've told you before, but I'd never seen her like this. Her eyes and teeth and entire face seemed to shine. But what she said then really made my warmed heart stop. "I know that," she said. "I've known it for a while."

Though she'd had her suspicions, Lisa said, she knew for sure last Sunday at the beach. To this day, I'm amazed at how much Lisa notices without ever letting on. She said she'd just been waiting for me to tell her. "The whole reason I wrote that letter," she said, "was to help you open up. That way, we can build our relationship on a foundation of truth."

I swear to God, those were the exact words she used.

"I think that's better, don't you?" she said with that same searing smile that made my insides sizzle. She said some other things too, but I don't remember what. I was so overwhelmed and in love with this girl that I didn't know what I was saying or what she was saying, or even who or where we were.

I must have told her there was something I wanted to show her in the shed, because that's where we ended up. There wasn't really anything I wanted to show her there at all. As soon as we got to where no one could see, I put my arms around her and gave her a kiss. I don't remember how many times I kissed her, but it was plenty. I hope I never forget that moment for the rest of my life, even though it's not very clear in my memory now. What I kept thinking was how good she smelled. I don't know what perfume or cologne she was wearing, but man did it smell good! We kissed for a long time, and she responded too. I kept thinking she would want to stop, but no, she was as into it as much as I was. I still had some glue on my upper lip, but Lisa didn't seem to care and, to tell you the truth, neither did I.

After a while, I thought we'd better stop kissing and talk about where to go from here. Lisa thought I should just keep coming over in my disguise, at least until her father eased her restriction. She was sure things would change soon. "Dad's already forgetting his worries about me and Lora getting pregnant," she said, smiling a knowing smile. "He's involved in some kind of business venture that's taking all his time and attention." Mrs. Hudson was usually gone too, Lisa said, and didn't seem to think about the twins much at all. "Sometimes I wish I had a real mom," Lisa sighed.

I told her my mother died when I was five, and I never even had a stepmom. This seemed to impress her. She put her arms around me and started kissing me again. Geese, how I loved this girl! It seemed like she couldn't get enough of me.

We agreed, however, on one thing that would be a challenge for both of us. And that was not to make it obvious at school that we liked each other. If it got around that we were in love, maybe Mr. and Mrs. Hudson would hear about it and try to stop us. We would see each other at school and say "Hi" and all, but we wouldn't really hang out together during passing periods or at lunch the way some couples do.

I wanted to go on kissing Lisa all afternoon, but feared someone would walk in on us, so I told her I was dying to taste one of her brownies. She laughed as we left the shed. Back at the table where we'd left lunch, I noticed a fly crawling on one sandwich. I ate that one myself, because I didn't want Lisa getting sick or dying or anything. We ate our lunch pretty much in silence. We looked at each other, making funny faces and laughing but saying very little.

"The brownies are perfect," I said when we had finished, and Lisa just laughed.

. . .

AFTER SHE LEFT, I WENT BACK TO WORK IN THE FLOWER beds. The place was looking good, if I may say so myself. By then it was about 3 p.m., and I thought I'd work for another 45 minutes or so, then clean up and go home. About 3:15 Lora and Paula came out of the house. I guess they'd been doing homework inside all afternoon. They were drinking Cokes or lemonades or iced tea or something. I don't remember exactly what. They were cutting up like crazy as usual, laughing their heads off. They really get along well together. They seemed like best friends, and that made me feel happy and warm inside, especially now that I'd told Lisa the truth and we had an understanding between us.

I was getting ready to call it quits when Lora got a call or something and went back into the house, leaving Paula alone. I wondered whether I should say something. He seemed deep in thought, and I couldn't tell whether he even knew I was there. I decided not to bother him.

I washed my hands with the garden hose and wiped them on my pants. Before entering the garage, I saw through the door that Mrs. Hudson's car was there. I looked behind me, trying to make eye contact with Paul, and there she stood—Mrs. Hudson herself—out there on the patio with him, apparently just having come from the house. She had a drink in one hand, probably a cocktail. The glass was tall, filled with orangish-red liquid. My brother was standing right next to her, and what I saw next really gave me a shock! Mrs. Hudson sort of leaned against Paul and rubbed her hand all over his rear, pinching it like a cushion. I figured I'd better turn around and get the hell out of there ASAP. I don't think either of them saw me.

Chapter Ten

Back home, I decided to talk to Paul. I had to. I didn't care whether he'd be busy with homework or whatever. The conversation was going to happen because I would insist. All I had to do was wait for him to get home.

Dad had eaten already and gone out to a movie. He'd left a note saying so. Dad seldom went out, especially with COVID all around and everything, but the theaters were just reopening and one of them was playing an old baseball movie I'd told him about called *The Natural* starring Robert Redford. Dad really is a sports nut, as I told you before. Anyway, there was a little movie theater in town that specialized in old films. Most of the stuff they featured you could probably find online, but I guess there are still people who only want to see their movies on big screens. And I guess you could say that my dad's one of them.

I think baseball is the greatest thing in the world. It sort of makes you feel proud to be an American, knowing it's an American sport and all. Basketball and football are American sports too. I know I'm really getting off the subject right now, but who cares? I just wanted you to know I like baseball movies, and because of that, so does my dad.

By now I was hungry again, so I made myself a peanut butter sandwich and poured a glass of milk. I thought about watching TV or listening to music, but didn't want to get too wrapped up in anything and miss Paul when he came in. So I just sat there in the living room, thinking. I don't remember exactly what I was thinking about, though I know my mind was buzzing. Pretty soon Paul came in, dressed like a guy now. I guess he'd changed down at the Bay in one of the public restrooms. There're a lot of weirdos down there who do strange things, so probably nobody even notices when Paul goes into the stall as a woman and comes out a man.

The minute Paul got through the front door, I told him we really needed to talk. To my great relief, he seemed to want to talk to me too. So, I told him I'd fix him a peanut butter sandwich or spaghetti or anything he wanted and then we would talk. "That sounds perfect!" Paul said, adding that he also wanted a cup of coffee because he had lots of studying to do and would probably be up all night. Paul never smoked or anything but drank coffee like a fiend.

Anyway, he wanted to tell me all about Lora, and what he said caught me completely off guard. "I told her all about the disguise," Paul said. "I told her I'm really Paul Santos." I don't think Lora was as sharp as Lisa, because Paul's disguise had completely fooled her. In fact, his news had shocked her like hell. Anyway, it didn't take Lora long to get the picture, and instead of getting mad and throwing a fit, she acted relieved. I guess when she found out, she started hugging and kissing him right there in the house, even though he still looked like a girl. "If anybody had seen us," Paul said, "they would have thought we were lesbians." Fortunately, no one did, so they planned to make other arrangements for all the kissing and hugging to come.

What really struck me as strange, though, was what Paul told me was going on in Lora's head. Apparently, they'd gone to her room to discuss all this in private after Paul first broke the news in the living room when nobody was there. I guess just before Paul told her the truth, Lora was having some deep psychological problems about what was happening to her. She was really in love with Paul Santos, I guess, but it was puppy love, if you know what I mean. She didn't think there was any way of getting to know Paul Santos and was trying to bury her feelings for him. And then something strange happened; she felt more and more attracted to her girlfriend, Paula. She wanted to be around Paula all the time, and when Paula wasn't there, she'd think about her so much that she was really feeling uncomfortable. Was she a lesbian? She'd never felt like this about any of her other girlfriends. At first, in fact, she'd been embarrassed to be around Paula because she was so big and sloppily dressed and her hair didn't look good at all. But Lora needed help with her homework, and Paula was always available. Then, as time went on, Paula had seemed to change. She put more effort into her appearance, and Lora could see that her face was beautiful. The only problem, really, was that her girth was too big for a girl.

Then Lora had a dream about Paula she found disturbing. She dreamed they were in the backyard talking and having a great time together like they usually did when, suddenly, Paula changed into a man who was kissing her and fondling her. They even found a grassy field somewhere where nobody could see them and ended up making love. Lora woke up feeling happy, which worried her even more. What was happening to her? She thought she was going insane.

Lora considered telling Paula not to come around anymore. In fact, she was planning on doing just that when Paul told her the truth and, well, literally made her dream come true. All except the part at the very end where they actually made love.

I guess they had a frank talk about sex right there in her bedroom, and Lora was the one who started it. She told Paul she really wanted to go to bed with him, the sooner the better. I think the fact that she'd been thinking about it longer than he had shocked the hell out of him. I know you don't know Paul like I do, but if you did, you'd believe his reaction was genuine. He just doesn't look at things the way most guys do. I wish I could explain it by telling you he's super religious or something, but the truth is he's not, although he believes in God and says he's a Christian and all. But he hardly ever goes to church.

Paul seemed a little depressed telling me all this. He didn't know exactly what to do about Lora. He wasn't afraid of getting VD or anything because she told him she's a virgin. But her getting pregnant would ruin both of their lives forever. In fact, he told me, it would break up their relationship if they started having sex and she had a kid. He was thinking about breaking off with Lora anyway, before things really got started. He had powerful feelings for her, and he admitted that some of them were sexual. But he wondered what kind of girl Lora was because she wanted to jump right in bed with him without even knowing him very well. He seemed so depressed that I changed the subject.

"OK," I said. "so what was Mrs. Hudson doing rubbing her hand all over your rear? I saw you guys on the patio."

He turned a little red. "That's embarrassing and I don't want to talk about it," my brother said.

But I was determined not to let him off the hook. "Talk to me, Paul," I commanded. "I won't tell a soul, I swear. You won't either, will you? I sure hope not."

So here's the story he told: Mrs. Hudson had the hots for Paul and saw through his disguise right away. "A woman knows things like that," she told him. "I can tell the difference between a man and a woman without even any clues." She didn't say anything to her husband, though, because if she blew the whistle, he would immediately send Paula home for good. And to tell the truth, Mrs. Hudson wanted Paula around, although she was jealous because she knew Paul was really after Lora.

I was even more surprised to hear what came next. It seems old man Hudson had the hots for Paula, too! Like the fool he was, he'd been completely taken in by the disguise. And probably because Mrs. Hudson wouldn't sleep with him, he started fantasizing about this new girl in his house night and day and decided to love up Paula if he could just find a way.

I could see what Paul was talking about now. All this was really disgusting. There was no doubting that. I can't imagine anyone over 40 making love with their wrinkled skin and sagging body parts and all. I was getting depressed myself now. I kept thinking about old Hudson's horrible breath.

Hudson tried to corner Paula twice to tell her what he was feeling. And, though the idea was disgusting, Paul felt the need to play up to the old man, even if just a little, for fear that he'd discover the truth and make him go home.

Mrs. Hudson found all this extremely amusing. She knew her husband was an old fool, of course, but now his foolishness seemed to reach additional dimensions that even she could never have imagined. "It's like watching a comedy taking place in my house," she told Paul. "If things got any better, I'll have to stop paying dues at the country club and spend more time at home."

But things were getting heavy with Mrs. Hudson too. Whenever she was home, she'd get Paul's ear. She made it plain that living with a complete turnoff like Mr. Hudson bored her almost to tears. If Paul would meet her just once at a hotel, she promised she wouldn't tell anyone his secret. "I'll even pay the bill and bring a picnic lunch," Mrs. Hudson said. "We'll have a good time, then you can do anything you want with that little bitch." It was obvious she was talking about Lora. All of which depressed Paul to no end. He clearly didn't know what to do. I'm sorry, but I couldn't help thinking of General George Custer standing on that hill with all those American Indians closing in on him. I didn't have any advice for Paul. I was just glad that it was *him* on that hill instead of me,

Chapter Eleven

I got up early the next morning because I couldn't sleep. It was Sunday, and I felt excited about what had happened with Lisa the day before. I started putting on my gardener's outfit and suddenly felt depressed. I couldn't bring myself to do it. I wished I was a normal guy and Lisa a normal girl, and I could just call her and take her out for a picnic or a movie or something. But then I thought of Paul and all he'd told me and started worrying about *him*. I guess thinking about movies put another idea in my head. Maybe Paul and I should take the day off and go to one together. We both wanted to see the latest Marvel film because lots of guys at school were talking about it. I went to Paul's room and knocked on the door. He was asleep. I guess he'd been up late doing homework as usual, but he didn't seem to mind that I'd roused him.

"Hey, how about going to the new Marvel flick with me today?" I suggested sticking my head in the door.

It was about 7:00 a.m. He liked the idea of taking the day off for a movie. He told me he and Lora had talked about doing the same thing, but he felt nervous about appearing with her in public dressed as a girl and, besides, Maria would have to go with them.

"This will give me a chance to calm down," my brother said.

I felt sorry for Lora and Lisa. Everywhere they went, either Maria or

Alihandro went along. It surprised me they didn't complain more, although they complained about it a little.

"I already checked the paper," I told Paul. "The movie starts at one."

He could spend the morning studying, I suggested, and I'd just knock around the house reading or whatever. "Don't forget to call Lora and tell her you won't be seeing her today," I reminded him. Can you imagine that? I sounded like his mother! I felt a little bad about that because he could think for himself and all, but I really felt worried about Paul just then. He didn't seem to be bugged by my being a mother hen.

"I'll call her as soon as I've showered," he promised.

That put another idea in my head. I should call Maria right away to tell her I was sick and wouldn't be coming to work that day. "Where do you keep Lora's number?" I asked Paul, realizing that he would naturally have it, being one of her "girlfriends" and all.

Anyway, Maria said that would be ok. "I don't see any problem with your missing the day," she said. "I'll tell Alihandro and Mr. Hudson." So I knocked around the house for a while, reading the paper, and even did some homework. I asked Paul if he wanted Steve to come along with us to the movie, and he said that would be fine. Steve was the fullback on our football team, who liked to hang out with us occasionally. So, I called him, and he said he would go.

He got to our house around 12:15 p.m., just after Paul and I had lunch. At 12:30, we started walking down toward the theater. The price of admission was way too high, but no one complained. You could save a lot of money by waiting for a movie to stream on TV. We weren't subscribed to too many streaming services, but Steve was and sometimes let us watch. The movie we were going to see today, though, wouldn't be streaming soon.

I really liked the movie, but it wasn't exactly what I thought it would be. It was a lot more violent, maybe even too much so. People had told me this, but I guess I wasn't prepared. The production, though, was very impressive, and the acting was great.

The thing is, though, I don't think I really had my mind on the movie. Don't get me wrong, I enjoyed being in the theater with my brother and Steve, but I kept wishing I was there with Lisa. I was feeling a little worried about not showing up at her house on the day after we'd had that big breakthrough in our relationship.

After the movie, we all went into the lobby to buy some candy and Coke. I think Steve and Paul were planning to sneak in to see another movie if they could. This was one of those theaters where they have all kinds of separate rooms and show different movies in them at various times. But I told them I wanted to go outside for a minute to catch a breath of fresh air.

What I really wanted was a smoke, which I figured I could have out front. I didn't care who saw me. I told the guys I would buy another ticket in a minute and come back in. Outside, the fresh air felt, well, *fresh*. I had to admit it was nicer down here by the beach. There was always a sweet breeze blowing, with very little smog. I reached into my pocket for cigarettes, but then had second thoughts. I know I like to come on all tough and everything, but I didn't want to get into trouble with the football coaches. They've told us many times that if they catch us smoking, they'll kick us off the team, and that's something I don't want.

I quickly forgot about smoking, though, because three other guys were standing right in front of me. It was one of Sandy's brothers and a couple of his friends. I wondered why they were hanging out around the movies. Somehow, I couldn't imagine them watching a Marvel Comics production. I feared them, but the thought of these three tough-acting losers sitting in there watching some Mickey Mouse movie with popcorn made me laugh.

"Hey, Santos," Sandy's brother said, "what's so funny? You think this is funny? I want to see you laugh when I kick your ass."

I wondered what they were doing on this side of town. And then I thought of Boy Jerome. Sandy's brother was saying something else, but I couldn't make it out. "Hey, Santos, are you listening to me?" he went on, this time clearly. "What do you say we step back out into the alley and settle old scores?"

It didn't pay to show any fear in front of these guys. And I really wasn't as scared of them as you might imagine because I'd brushed up against them before and knew that I could take any of them one-on-one with little trouble at all. To be honest, though, I was a little scared because I didn't know if I could handle them all together at once, especially if they had knives and guns and all. You never want to underestimate these guys, though usually they fought with only their fists.

"All right," I said, "I'd be happy to take you guys on, but one at a time and none of us are going to use knives or anything. Agreed?"

That seemed all right with them. Paul and I had developed a sign that we'd use when one of us was in trouble so we could ask for help while saying nothing. Anyway, I made the sign now behind my back. I really hate to tell you what it was because it was the finger. Paul and I didn't go around giving people the finger, so we reserved it for times of trouble like this. Anyway, I made the sign behind my back, hoping that Paul and Steve were in the theater's lobby somewhere where they could see me. There was no way of telling whether they had seen the sign. I was afraid to look behind me.

The guys led me down the street and around the corner. They were ahead of me and didn't seem to be worried that I'd turn around and run away or anything. Believe me, the thought crossed my mind, but I didn't run. I kept hoping that something would end this confrontation before it started. I was getting sick of worrying about them popping up on me like this. I wanted to get them out of my life forever because I didn't feel like I had any connection with them anymore.

We got to the alley, and I wondered how these guys knew their way around this theater so well. We walked down the alley to a little cul-de-sac behind the theater. There was lots of trash out there, and it was really a mess. The trash cans stood full to the brim with junk spilling out of them all over the place. It was a totally suitable spot to meet guys just like the ones I was meeting, if you know what I mean.

Two of them quickly moved around behind me and grabbed my arms. Then Sandy's brother pulled out a knife. Apparently, these guys didn't intend to play fair. Suddenly I felt scared as hell and didn't know what to do. I feared Paul and Steve hadn't seen my sign.

But I had to do something. My adrenaline was pumping. I kicked hard at Sandy's brother, missing the spot I was aiming for but tapping him on the upper thigh. He let out a muffled sound, and I elbowed the other two guys in the ribs as hard as I could, just like I'd seen in the movies. I guess I hit hard enough to force them to let go, but one guy still had a hold of my shirt and ripped it pretty good. The other one lost his grip entirely and was trying to jump on my back. He hit me in the back of the head, but then fell off. I was free now and started running out of the cul-de-sac as fast as I could to get away. I'll be damned if I'm going to fight three guys with knives using nothing but my fists. I hope you don't think I'm chicken or something, but I really don't care if you do. I'm not exactly stupid.

That's when I saw my brother and Steve coming around the corner. I was running so fast I bumped right into them and kept going for a few more yards before I could stop and turn around. They didn't stop at all but kept on running towards my attackers. Suddenly, my brother picked up a heavy trash can and smashed it down on top of one guy, throwing him to the ground. He kept hitting him over and over, though it soon became apparent that the guy had had enough. Steve, meanwhile, was kicking Sandy's brother, who apparently had dropped the knife. I think Steve had taken a course in karate or something and thought he was The Rock. And even though as many kicks were missing as hitting, I could see that he was doing a pretty good job kicking the stuffing out of that asshole now also on the ground.

One of the other guys tried running past me to get away, but I grabbed him and pushed him up against the wall of the theater. Then I punched him in the stomach a few times, grabbed a big gob of his hair and banged his head against the wall. But I could see that he was only trying to get away. There was no way this kid was my age; he must have been a couple years younger. Now his face bore a look of absolute terror. He knew I could kill him if I wanted. I started feeling sorry for him, realizing that he just wanted to get away. So, I let go, and for a minute he just stood there, not knowing what to do. Then he started slowly backing away. When I didn't react, he turned around and ran like hell, rounding the corner to disappear.

I saw what the other guys were doing. Maybe they needed some help or something. Paul was still banging the trashcan on the guy, who by now was a bloody mess. I guess some of the metal on the can had gotten torn up and was razor sharp because one of the kid's ears was now hanging by a flimsy piece of skin. Steve had his man down now and was kicking him repeatedly in the head and stomach and butt and anywhere else he could land a kick. Sandy's brother was trying to take it like a man, but I could see that he was in lots of pain and doing his best to protect his private parts. He was holding himself there, rolling around to deflect the kicks.

I felt terrified now that my guys wouldn't stop until they'd killed someone. My adrenaline flow had slowed by then and I was trying to think as straight as I could. We'd really be in big trouble if one of these guys wound up dead. I shouted for Paul and Steve to stop, but they didn't seem to hear. I decided the guy Paul was working over was probably in the worst shape, so I grabbed at the trashcan, but it just cut my hand. Later, it took 15 stitches to sew it up. But when Paul saw the cut, he stopped swinging and put down the can. My cut looked worse than it was. Paul didn't say anything, just sort of looked at me as if to say he was sorry. But his eyes still looked wild.

"Paul, we better stop Steve from kicking anymore!" I said. I didn't have to explain. Immediately Paul grabbed Steve, yelling that the fight was over. Steve calmed down a bit, but lost control of his mouth. He called Sandy's brother every name in the book and told him he'd kick his butt if he ever showed up in that part of town again.

By this time, Sandy's brother was picking himself up off the concrete and helping his compadre to his feet. That guy could hardly walk and blood covered him like a splotchy blanket. Believe me, I almost felt like puking. They moved out of the cul-de-sac and into the alley. Steve was still shouting insults, and I expected one of them to turn around and say something like they'd get us later or they'd remember this, and we'd better watch out or whatever. But they didn't say a thing. And once again I felt fear about how badly we'd hurt these guys.

When they were gone, the three of us shouted as if we had just won the Super Bowl. Until then, Paul had just stood there dumbly, as if he didn't know what was happening. But now he shouted his head off with Steve and me. I don't know why we did that; we just did.

We didn't even consider going back into the theater after that. The fight had messed us up, and we were feeling high in victory. As we walked home, we acted all macho and shit like we were the greatest fighters in the world, and I was into it just as much as they were. I'll admit that. But I felt a little embarrassed, even though no one who saw me would know it. I don't know why guys act that way, they just do.

As we walked home, I remembered thinking about Paul. I didn't really care how Steve acted, but Paul mattered and there was one thing about him that really worried me. Paul doesn't often get into fights, but when he does get into one, he seems to enjoy it. He doesn't talk very much afterwards. I think he would have killed that guy if I hadn't intervened. This wasn't the first time I'd noticed this in him, there were other times too. Was my brother a steely eyed, cold-blooded killer? I don't know, but he just doesn't seem able to stop once he gets started. And I don't mind saying that it scares the hell out of me.

Chapter Twelve

There isn't very much to tell about the next couple of months. Paul and I kept up our disguises and went over to Lisa's and Lora's house on the weekends. Sometimes Paul even went there during the week after football practice in the evening. Now that the girls knew the score, we didn't have to take so many pains hiding stuff from them. Our key problem was finding secret places to talk to one another or hold hands or kiss or whatever. After a while, Paul and I let each girl in on what was going on with the other. With everybody on the same page, everything went more smoothly.

But this was just the quiet before the storm because soon all hell broke loose, as I will tell you now. My story first. One Saturday, working in the flower beds around the house, I had a feeling something strange was about to happen. I'm not trying to make you think I'm psychic or anything because I'm not, but everyone in the household seemed silent and tense. Eventually, I found out why; the Department of Homeland Security had finally caught up with Alihandro and taken him downtown. Lisa told me that Maria and the kids were down there trying to get him out.

And then something even stranger happened. I saw it while taking a break by the shed where I like to stretch out once in a while after spending a long time bent over pulling weeds. What I saw really gave me a start: old Hudson, all dressed up in a business suit and holding a briefcase, singing his head off. I don't know what he was singing because I don't know many old songs. I could see all this because the door at the back of the garage was open, and so was the garage door at the front of the house. Hudson was singing and skipping at the same time. I'm not kidding. I think he was still skipping when a cab pulled up. He got in and kept on singing as he closed the cab door behind him.

I figured he was going on a business trip or something. But then I remembered that Hudson only went on business trips during the week. He made a point of not going on the weekends. He didn't have to travel on the weekends because he was so high in the corporation that he could do as he pleased. In fact, Lisa had told me it was one of Hudson's principles not to go on business trips during the weekends. I was thinking about this when something even stranger happened. Mrs. Hudson, who was home, started leaving too. She had spruced herself up pretty good, even more than usual. After climbing into her Mercedes, she drove away. I could tell she was in a hurry because she laid a little rubber out on the street in front of the house, something adults seldom do.

I walked back to the flower beds next to the house, wondering what was going on. It wasn't strange for Mrs. Hudson to leave because she was leaving all the time. What was strange, though, was for her to leave when there were no other adults around. Lisa, Lora and Paul were in the house, with no one there to watch them!

Then I started thinking about all that could happen. Things had been going well with Lisa over the past couple of months. We'd done lots of kissing and talking, and we'd even sort of felt around here and there, if you know what I mean. I'm too embarrassed to tell you the details. But I had a pretty good idea that, should the opportunity present itself, Lisa would go all the way. It was strange because I didn't mind taking my time with her. Most girls are fast these days, and I guess it doesn't take long to get what you want. But with Lisa, it was different. We were taking our time because there were always adults around, which was kind of nice, if you can imagine that. It was sort of relaxing because there wasn't any pressure. I've heard that's the way it was in the old days; people just took their time. Maybe the kids had more fun back then, after all.

But now I was getting other thoughts in my head and figured if I could reach out to Paul, maybe we could work something out. We'd have to do it before the adults got home, though. I'd heard that these things take a long time at the DHS, and Maria had gotten on the bus with the kids about half an hour before. It would take her at least three hours to get there and back. Old Hudson was probably on a business trip and would be gone all weekend, and once Mrs. Hudson got to the country club, she never returned until after I went home at four or five in the evening.

Then something happened that really blew my mind. I was working close to the house near the den with its sliding glass door open and could hear what was going on in inside. The phone rang, and Lora answered it. "Oh, no!" she said, or something like that. Then she said they'd be right there, and she and Paul bolted out of the house, got into the Chrysler, and drove away. Paul sat at the wheel dressed like a girl, as usual. I knew all this happened because I heard it, and actually *saw* them drive away. I even tried to catch them to find out what was going on, but didn't get there in time.

This left Lisa alone in the house. Imagine that! So, I shut the garage doors, both the big one and the little one, and locked them tight. Then I walked into Lisa's room, but she was taking a shower. I could hear the water running. I went to the front door to lock it too, and when I got back, Lisa's was just coming out of the shower wrapped in a towel. She regarded me with a puzzled look on her face.

"We're alone in the house," I said, hoping she would understand.

She got the message immediately, smiled and, I swear, dropped her towel to the floor. God, I've beheld nothing more beautiful in my life! I'd seen her in a bathing suit and felt around a bit like I told you before. But I'd never seen her stark naked until this moment and felt like I was about to faint. I tugged at my clothes to get them off and, frankly, had a difficult time. It seemed like it was taking ages. Lisa didn't appear to be shy or ashamed of her body at all and wasn't hiding any part of it. I know it took me a while to get my clothes off because I literally couldn't take my eyes off her. I guess I was afraid if I looked away, she'd disappear. As I tugged at my clothes, she just stood there, all naked and beautiful in her short-wet blond hair, laughing with her bright blue eyes flashing at me like stars. Finally my clothes lay in a crumpled heap at my feet, and I stood there as naked as Lisa.

I'll spare you the details. Let's just say that we made love right there on the bed in her bedroom. It felt like we fit together perfectly, if you know what I mean. I think that's all I should say about it. Neither of us thought of taking any precautions or anything. I think we both were afraid someone might walk in any minute. And we didn't say much either, as if there were a tape recorder somewhere in the house that could hear any sound we made.

Afterwards, I put my clothes back on as fast as I could and went right outside. I picked up the hand trowel and pretended to be working in the flower beds, although it must have been obvious that I wasn't getting much done. I kept thinking about what a nice time I'd had with Lisa, but then started feeling depressed because, now that I'd gotten what I wanted so much, where would we go from here? From the moment I first saw her picture in the trophy case, I'd wanted to make love to Lisa. But now I felt like I'd gone all the way with the wrong girl. It wasn't that I wanted some other girl, that wasn't it at all. It was just that I felt like I'd made a mistake, that I shouldn't have done all that with Lisa. It just didn't seem right. She was the girl with whom I should have saved it for later, when we were properly married. What would we do now? She made love to me as if she thought I knew what was going on in life, like I was some older guy who knew the ropes and all. Now I felt kind of scared that she trusted me so much when, really, I didn't know any more about what would or should happen than anybody else.

Pretty soon, Lisa came out of the house. By then she was dressed, but I don't remember anything about what she was wearing. We talked a while, but I don't remember what it was about, so it mustn't have been that important. I remember, though, that we didn't talk about what had just happened in the bedroom. I could tell that neither of us knew how to handle it, so we just didn't bring it up. We both wondered where Mr. and Mrs. Hudson and Paul and Lora had gone, but we didn't talk about that too much, either. We knew that Alihandro and Maria and their kids were down at the DHS, like I told you before.

After about half an hour, I told Lisa I'd better get back to work. You might think it weird of me to worry about giving Hudson a fair shake for the little he was paying. Perhaps it was guilt, because I felt especially that way after having had my way with his daughter. But I must not really be such a good guy after all, because 30 minutes later, I was ready to say to hell with the work and go back for another poke. In fact, I almost walked right into the house again as if I owned the place, but something held me back. I felt like maybe I'd gone too far already; that maybe something terrible would happen if I pushed things too far and too fast.

The truth, though, was that I wasn't getting much work done, anyway. So around 2 p.m. I decided to go on home and wait for Paul. I wanted to be honest, so wrote on the time sheet I kept that I'd left at two. Then I knocked on the back door, and Lisa opened it.

"Any news on where everybody went and what's going on?" I asked.

"Not yet," she said, looking a little worried.

I told her I was knocking off for the day and going home. She just kissed me on the lips, said goodbye, and closed the door.

Back home, I had nothing to do but kill time until Paul arrived. Dad sat watching a game on TV, and the house was all dark inside as usual. I said hello to him, marched straight to my room and tried to go to sleep but couldn't.

An hour later, I called Lisa. She sounded really worried now, because she still hadn't heard anything and didn't know what was going on. I called her twice more that afternoon, and the second time it sounded like she was crying. In fact, she was sobbing so hard she could hardly even talk. Lora had called from the hospital, Lisa said between sobs, and told her that their father had a heart attack. They didn't know whether he would live or die. In fact, she said he'd been pronounced dead on arrival, but then the doctors had revived him. Now he lay hooked up to all kinds of machines, and they didn't know whether surgery would work.

"Do you need me to take you to the hospital?" I asked, already wondering how we would get there.

"Actually," she said, "my mom asked me to stay home and watch the house."

"Do you want me to come over?"

"Thank you, Michael," she said softly, "but I really think I need some time alone. I'll call you tomorrow, or just see you Monday at school."

As much as I wanted to be with her, I respected her wishes. I'd been a little kid when my mother died and hadn't really known what was going on. So, I don't know what it's like to stand by, while a parent lies at death's door."

"Can I keep calling you?" I asked.

"Sure," she said, which made me feel a little better. Then we both got off the phone.

I called her a few more times that day, and at first, she didn't have any additional information. The last time I called was 7:30 p.m., and by then she'd called the hospital herself. Mr. Hudson was in serious but stable condition, she said, and would undergo open heart surgery in the morning. They'd told Lisa his chances were pretty good, and she seemed a little calmer and wasn't crying like before.

About an hour later, Paul came home, now dressed as himself. I couldn't imagine him coming home as Paula because that would require a lot of explaining and we were trying to keep Dad in the dark. Paul invited me into his bedroom. He had something important to tell me, he said, that just couldn't wait.

"I'm really in trouble," my brother said as soon as he'd shut the door. I'd never seen him in such a panic. "Mr. Hudson is in the hospital near death," he said, "and I'm the one to blame."

"What?" I said, not comprehending. "I know he's in the hospital, but how is it your fault? I saw him leave this morning, but you and Lora didn't leave until later."

Then he told me the whole story. I guess things had been getting increasingly uncomfortable for him in the Hudson house. Both the old man and Mrs. Hudson had been pressuring him for secret rendezvous, as I told you before. Paul had put them off as long as possible, but then Mrs. Hudson threatened to tell her husband the truth unless Paul met her somewhere for sex. She promised that would be the end of it and afterwards she wouldn't tell.

Paul had been obsessing about it all week until, finally, he'd come up with a plan. He wasn't sure it would work, Paul said, but was desperate enough to try anything. So, he'd arranged to meet Mrs. Hudson at a sleazy hotel *that very morning*. He gave Mrs. Hudson the address and told her to rent room number seven. If that room wasn't available, he'd instructed, she should call Lora and make up a reason for her to mark a date on the calendar, the same number as the room she had rented. That way, if Lora got a call, Paul would know the room number and, if not, well, it would be number seven. Then, about an hour after she left the house, Paul would make up some excuse to go home, but really go to the hotel room.

But that was only part of the plan. One evening during the week, Paul, posing as Paula, had talked privately with Mr. Hudson. He told the old man to meet him—or *her*—at the same hotel he'd told Mrs. Hudson about. Paula would rent the room herself—it would be number seven—and Hudson could reimburse her later. She told Hudson to leave the house as if he were going on a business trip, but really take the cab to the park down the street to wait for Paula's call.

Paula then wrote down Mr. Hudson's cell number and told him he'd call with an update if room seven wasn't available. If Hudson hadn't heard from her by 12:30 p.m., my brother instructed, he should take another cab to the hotel where he would find Paula waiting for him in—you guessed it—room number seven.

I know all this sounds ridiculous, but Hudson was too busy listening to ask questions. When Paula finished, the old man repeated everything almost verbatim to make sure he'd gotten it right. That surprised Paula, who figured if he wanted Hudson to go to hell and back before showing up at that sleazy hotel, well, the old man would do it. "Sleazy" is the word Paul kept using to describe the place. I don't use it much myself, though I know what it means.

Anyway, Hudson ate the plan up like pizza. He seemed as excited as a kid. He told Paula not to worry about him being old because he would get some of his wife's cocaine, which would "perk" him right up, if you know what I mean. I guess it's some kind of aphrodisiac, or something, like Viagra.

But it seems the old man's heart just couldn't take Mrs. Hudson answering his knock at room seven, especially since he was so excited about seeing Paula and all doped up on his wife's drugs. Mrs. Hudson told Paul all about it later at the hospital. She said old Hudson didn't know what to do when she let him into the hotel room. Apparently, Mrs. Hudson had played it cool by pretending she'd found out what he was up to and was heading him off at the pass. I guess Hudson couldn't think of a way to explain why he was knocking on the door of a sleazy hotel room, so just sort of staggered in not saying anything, sat down on the bed breathing hard and had a heart attack.

At first, she thought he was faking it. That made her really mad because she'd already come up with a really cool lecture to deliver on the spot, but now he wasn't even listening. She felt like marching right over to the bed and slapping him in the face. But then he got all blue, stopped breathing and fell forward to the floor, stretched out there motionless like some discarded puppet.

Mrs. Hudson panicked. She ran down to the hotel lobby and called the paramedics. They came right away and hooked old Hudson up to some oxygen or something. I don't remember if Paul told me they gave him a shot or pounded on his chest or whatever. But they took him to the hospital right away and pronounced him dead on arrival, as I told you before. Then they brought him around, he got a little better, and they planned on operating the very next morning.

Mrs. Hudson was furious at Paul for playing this trick on her, but he honestly didn't know whether it would go better for him if Mr. Hudson lived or if he died. In fact, he thought she might even thank him if her husband died.

And that brings me to the end of my story. Right now, I'm sitting on the hill near that hospital where Lisa is. Remember the place up near Santa Barbara where they sent her after discovering she was pregnant? I come up here every weekend, like I told you before, and stay with an old friend at the nearby university. If you want to know how I have the time to do that, well, it's because I had to drop out of school and now work at a gas station. I'm not even employed at the beauty shop anymore. Lisa had to drop out of school too in order to come up here. Her parents are thinking about sending her to some prep school for girls back East next year. I guess neither of us will graduate on time with friends our own age.

I'm really getting ahead of myself because there's a bit more I should tell you. Old Hudson pulled through all right. The day after his "accident" they did a double bypass on him or something. Or maybe it was a triple bypass or stent, for all I know. Sorry, I don't know much about heart surgery. Whatever they did to him, though, I guess the old guy is doing great now. He feels much better than before the operation. Somehow he and Mrs. Hudson seem to get along better too, though nobody knows why. Mrs. Hudson doesn't talk much to Paul anymore now that her husband knows Paul isn't Paula but Paul Santos. Mrs.

Hudson still hangs out at the country club but seems a lot more affectionate around the old man than she used to be. They sleep in the same room now, even under the same covers. No one knows why things are better at the Hudson house, they just are. Who can understand what adults do, anyway? Heck, I never understood how an old man like Mr. Hudson could get together with a hot young woman like Mrs. Hudson.

You probably want to know what happened between Paul and the Hudsons after Mr. Hudson found out about his little trick and that he wasn't a girl. You probably think he got into all kinds of trouble and will never see their daughter again. That's what I thought would happen too, but it didn't. In fact, it's just the opposite. For a while everything stayed quiet while old Hudson took it easy to recover from his surgery. Paul didn't dare go over there for fear of what Mrs. Hudson would do.

Pretty soon, though, Lora called him up and said her parents wanted to talk. He asked her what it was about, but she just told him not to worry and come right on over. So, Paul beat back his fear and went on over. When he got there, they had a family powwow. Lisa told me all about it because she was there too.

"Lora spilled the beans to Mom and Dad about Paul," Lisa said. "She told them everything."

The weird thing, though, is that Mr. Hudson had listened and decided that maybe Paul wasn't such a poor catch for his daughter after all. Paul can be very impressive, especially when people hear he's going to Stanford. Anyway, I guess after old Hudson came close to death and got his internal plumbing cleaned, he started seeing things differently and behaved differently, too. In some strange way, Lisa said, he was like a new man.

At this family talk, apparently, the Hudsons let it all hang out and told their daughters the truth about what was going on. The girls would soon be adults, they said, and should know that adults can make mistakes too. At first, what they said shocked the sisters. But then they started feeling better about their parents than they had before. I know it must be hard to learn that your own parents are up to the things that Mr. and Mrs. Hudson were, but Lora and Lisa weren't exactly acting like perfect little daughters, either. Everybody in the Hudson house, in fact, didn't exactly like what they were finding out about everybody else.

I think they all decided it was better to finally tell the truth than to lie continuously about everything.

So, what about Paul? I'm sure the Hudsons were really embarrassed about their shenanigans with him and probably figured things might even get worse if they kicked him out and never let him see their daughter again. If they let him go away angry, they probably thought he'd tell somebody what happened and go after revenge. I don't know. But if that's the way it was, that's not how it came across at all. I think Paul really impressed them, especially with his Puritanical attitude about sex and all. You know how Paul can handle adults. That he wasn't interested in having sex with Lora must have really sounded like good news to them. So, they stopped the restriction as long as she was dating Paul.

So now, if you can believe it, Paul doesn't have to wear a dress. He and Lora can even go out alone, without Maria tagging along! There was a lot more to this family conversation, of course, but that's what it boiled down to. I'm practically in shock. To think that Paul was in so much trouble with the Hudsons and embarrassed them so much, and yet ended up with their blessings, well, it's just unbelievable!

I especially can't believe it after what's happened to *me*. I'm on the blacklist at the Hudson house right now. It seems unfair as hell, but whoever said the world was fair? I guess I'm really to blame because I'm a creep after all. I know it, the Hudsons know it, and everybody knows it because it's the truth.

Anyway, I guess Lisa was ready to tell her parents about what she'd been up to, hoping to get herself off restriction like her sister, but then had second thoughts. It happened after the subject of Paul's strict attitude towards sex came up, and she started feeling guilty about being a lot more involved with me than Lora was with Paul, if you know what I mean. So, Lisa decided not to say anything until she could talk to me. And when we finally did talk, we basically decided to go on as we were. I would still be Manuel the gardener until we came up with a better plan. Oh, I almost forgot to tell you, but they deported Alihandro. Everybody thinks he'll be able to come back just as soon as he gets things straightened out at home. In the meantime, Maria and the kids still live with the Hudsons.

Anyway, we didn't know what we'd do, and then the worst thing happened to me that could ever happen. I found out about it one

Saturday morning when Lisa came out to the backyard looking all happy. "What's up?" I asked, curious about what was causing her to smile.

"We have to talk," she said,.

"Ok, I'm here. What do we have to talk about?"

"I'm pregnant," she blurted, still smiling with, well, pregnant expectation.

"What?" I replied, not sure I'd heard her correctly.

"I missed a few periods," Lisa said, "so Maria took me to the doctor. Isn't that exciting?"

I couldn't believe what I was hearing, especially that she actually felt all happy about it and expected me to be overjoyed too. She pretty quickly found out otherwise. She was going on and on about how we could get married and work part-time and finish school and all. Then she'd go to college because she didn't want to give up on that, and I didn't have to go to college if I didn't want to. Daddy wouldn't be too mad if we'd just tell him the truth, and he'd probably help us out a little financially because he had so much money. I don't know everything she said because I wasn't listening too carefully. I just kept on saying to myself, "Holy shit, holy shit, holy shit..."

Pretty soon she stopped talking, looked at me brightly, and wanted to know what I thought. "Lisa," I said, "have you considered getting an abortion?"

I guess that was the wrong thing to say because the brightness left Lisa's face, and she suddenly got very quiet. It was as if the ice age had descended again, and it felt much colder outside than it had just a minute before. Lisa started crying. "It really hurts that you would think of killing something that's part of both of us," she mumbled, or words to that effect. "Especially something as precious as a baby. I thought you loved me more than that. I guess I don't know you so well after all"

Then she turned and ran into the house before I could even respond.

That was on a Saturday, so I finished up early and went home. I didn't know what to do. I thought of calling Lisa and trying to patch things up, but in truth, I wasn't sure that I really wanted to patch things up.

The next day, I called Maria and told her I wouldn't be coming to work because I felt sick and had a pile of homework to do. The part about feeling sick was true. Instead of doing homework, though, I called Marty and asked if we could take a walk on the beach and then go to a movie. She agreed to meet me downtown. I didn't want to pick her up at her house because I might run into Jerome or Sandy's brother or somebody and knew I couldn't deal with it on that day. So, I drove Dad's car downtown and met Marty at the agreed time and place.

You're probably wondering why I never talk much about cars like most teenagers do. I guess I'm not really into cars, and not a typical teenager in this respect. I own an old Ford Mustang which is sitting on cinder blocks in my garage. Dad parks his car out on the street. This Mustang always seemed to break down, and I really don't enjoy working on cars much. And keeping it up was getting pretty expensive, not to mention buying the gas and paying insurance. Dad refused to pay because he couldn't afford it. And I could see that I'd have to drop out of school and get a job just to keep that car going. So, instead, I let the thing sit there on the street in the old neighborhood until we moved. We ended up towing it to our new apartment near the beach. Since they have different rules here about leaving cars on the street, we hauled the thing into the garage and left it sitting there. Dad lets me drive his car now and then, so I can get around all right. Paul has no interest in cars because he's all concerned about going to Stanford now and doesn't want a car until after graduation.

Anyway, I took Dad's car to pick up Marty. He would just have to get over to visit Mom's grave on his own that day. Marty looked the same. We headed down to the beach, and there were plenty of parking places there because it wasn't warm anymore. We walked up and down the water line for quite a while. I wanted to tell her what was happening with me and Lisa but didn't. We talked a lot about the things we used to do and all that, but I don't really remember exactly what we talked about because my mind was far away.

Then we went to the movies, and I don't even remember what we saw. I remember one thing, though, and that was that there were lots of good-looking girls there and I really checked them out. It didn't matter that I was there with Marty, and it seemed like my thing with Lisa was over anyway, so, of course, I started noticing other girls. The ones who weren't pregnant. When the idea of pregnancy entered my mind, I started feeling really depressed and felt like a jerk for checking out all the good-looking girls in the theater.

After the movie, I took Marty back downtown. I don't remember what we talked about in the car. In fact, I don't remember much at all about being with Marty, just that I was with her and felt guilty about noticing all the good-looking, non-pregnant girls.

From that point on, everything seems like a blur. I kept working at the Hudsons' on weekends, feeling unhappy as hell about everything that had happened. My grades went down, football season was over, and I had no thoughts of going out for baseball that year. I really didn't care about school, or baseball, or even Lisa anymore. I just remember being miserable all the time, and not knowing what to do about it.

I sent Lisa a couple of notes. Maria took them to her, but no answers came back. I didn't really care if she answered or not. I truly didn't, but kept on working at the Hudson house anyway. Paul and I didn't talk much. I think he was so happy being able to openly date Lora that he didn't even notice what was going on in my life. He probably thought, or hoped, that I was doing just fine when I wasn't at all.

Pretty soon, of course, the Hudsons found out that Lisa was pregnant. Mrs. Hudson noticed first because in April or so Lisa really started showing, and there was no way to hide it any longer. It didn't take them too long to pull her out of school and send her up to the home for unwed mothers where I am right now.

Eventually I quit at the Hudsons. One morning I just called Maria and told her I was done without saying why. She probably already knew about everything, anyway. I just told her I quit with no explanation and hung up right away. I started skipping school a lot and didn't do much at home in the evenings except listen to music. On the weekends, I just hung around the house or took walks on the beach.

I can't tell you I tried to commit suicide, or started drinking too much, or took dope, or got into a car accident because none of those things happened. I didn't even care enough to get into trouble. But after about a month of floating around doing nothing, I actually started caring again. Just a little at first, then more and more. I got a job at a gas station because I needed the money to drive up the coast on weekends, and I started buying some things for the baby to keep in my room. I even found a little store where they had nothing but baby stuff. All of it was expensive, but they were nice and gave me advice on what to buy for an infant. Every time I'd go in there, they'd ask me how the baby was, and I'd make up all sorts of stuff about the health of the mother and all. And as funny as this may sound to you, all the lies started helping me feel better. In fact, I cared a little more every day.

That's when I saw a psychiatrist. I had enough money left over after going back and forth to Santa Barbara and buying all that stuff for the baby, so I made an appointment with someone I found online. It was expensive, but I had to talk to someone, and I think the psychiatrist did me some good. He suggested I try to write what happened on paper and share it with him for a few minutes each time we met. What you're reading now, in fact, resulted from that suggestion.

I tried to get in touch with Lisa by getting the attention of a guard at the place she was staying. I gave him 25 dollars to deliver a letter I'd written about what I was up to and all that had happened. In it, I asked Lisa, sincerely now, to please forgive me because I loved her and the baby and wanted us to get married as soon as she got out of that place. I told her we'd graduate from high school, and I'd get a job to save enough to send her to college. We wouldn't have to ask Mr. Hudson for a penny, we'd do it all ourselves.

I rented some binoculars to see whether Lisa ever came out into the yard of that place. And I rented long lenses and cameras to get a picture of her if she did come out. I even got this high-powered telescope kind of thing to bring her right up close, but I never saw her.

Finally, one day, the guard came to the fence near where I was and said he had a letter for me. I gave him a 10-dollar bill, and he handed it over. It was from Lisa. I opened the envelope, and there were two pictures inside, both of a tiny baby. I think it was the same baby, but I couldn't really be sure. The first one showed a baby all messy-looking and bloody and crying its head off, making a terrible face. The baby was naked, and I could see it was a girl. The second picture showed a baby all cleaned up and wrapped in a blanket. The blanket was yellow, and the baby was in a pink layette. I knew the word "layette" because I'd been talking to the people down at the baby shop quite a bit lately about baby things. This baby was sleeping peacefully. I turned the pictures over, but Lisa had written nothing on their backs. There was a piece of paper in the envelope. It was a letter from her. Here's what it said:

Dear Michael:

Here are two pictures of our daughter. She was born last night. She doesn't have a name because I have to give her up. I've been told that some really nice people have adopted her. Both Daddy and I think this is the best thing to do. I'm sure you'll agree too when you look at all of this objectively and think about everything that's happened.

I hope you'll save the pictures because those are the only ones I have of her. If they find them here, they'll take them away. A young nurse trainee took them when no one was around. She would lose her job if they knew she did it. I appreciate what she did and hope you will take care of the pictures and not let them get into the wrong hands.

As far as our relationship goes, I haven't made up my mind. I've been going through so much in this hospital that I haven't really had much time to think about you. I'm not even sure I love you anymore. I guess time will tell. Right now, I'm not saying we will get back together, and I'm not saying we won't. Let's just wait and see, ok?.

I hope you are doing well. I am all right, and will go home pretty soon, but I'm not sure exactly when.

Lisa

I read the letter over and over. I held up the paper against the sunlight and could tell that Lisa had let her tears drop on it. You could tell because there were some spots that looked roundish and wrinkled like water had gotten on the paper. I stared at the two pictures of our little baby girl, who we would never hold. Then I felt my own cheeks and knew that I was crying too. And that's all I remember now and all I can say.

--The End--

About the Author

D. Ron Featheringill is a retired college professor and high school English teacher with many years of experience in understanding the rhythms of literature and the problems of teenagers. Having deep roots in the Native American and Hispanic communities of Southern California, he is well-equipped to interpret and express the pathos, joys, contradictions, and satisfactions of living in the worlds they inhabit. Featheringill is the author of The Tension Between Diving Will and Human Free Will in Milton and the Classical Epic Tradition (Peter Lang, 1990).

David Haldane is an award-winning journalist, author, and radio broadcaster whose previous books include Nazis & Nudists (2015), Jenny on the Street (2021) and A Tooth in My Popsicle (2023). A former staff writer for the Los Angeles Times, where he contributed to two Pulitzer Prize-winning stories, Haldane currently divides his time between homes in Joshua Tree, California, and Northern Mindanao, Philippines, where he writes a weekly column for The Manila Times. David and Ron have been best friends since their high school.

Made in the USA
Monee, IL
16 December 2024